# Desert Blood

*Book 2*
*The Wolves of Twin Moon Ranch*

by Anna Lowe

TWIN MOON PRESS

# Contents

# Other books in this series

visit www.annalowebooks.com

# Free Book

*Desert Wolf*

Get your free e-book now!

Sign up for my newsletter at *annalowebooks.com* to get your free copy of *Desert Wolf* (Book 1.1 in the series).

Lana Dixon may have won her destined mate's heart, but that was in Arizona. Now, she's bringing her desert wolf home to meet her family — the sworn enemies of his pack. How far will they push her mate to prove himself worthy? And is their relationship ready for the test?

# Chapter One

Fleeing wasn't the hard part; knowing when to stop was. But how far was far enough? How fast?

Heather didn't know. All she cared about was getting away. Red-eyed and bleary, stretched beyond exhaustion, she drove until the thick woods and hills of the East gave way to the infinite landscape of the West, with no plan but to get away from the beast who lusted after her blood.

She nearly rushed through this barren landscape entirely, a mere blip on a map she had long since given up on following. But from one mile to the next, the frantic urge to run was replaced by a warm, safe sensation, as if she'd flipped a shower tap from icy cold to blissfully hot. She let her dusty orange VW roll to a stop on the side of the road then got out and turned in a slow circle, scanning the scene. What was it about this place?

The sun rose boldly over the high altitude desert, highlighting a razorback horizon wrinkled by time. A pale crescent moon hung low over the hills, dripping pale pink light on the brush below. All of it was perfumed by sage and pine, beargrass and buttercup. The grandeur of the scene spoke of time—eons of it, whispering on a breath of wind.

This. This was the place. Even with her eyes closed, she could feel the rightness of it. This place would become her home.

A falcon wheeled overhead, and its sharp cry split the air. Heather blinked, snapping herself back to reality. Wait—there was no home. There was only escape. But for now, this would have to do. No use in running blindly any more. She needed to make a plan, to think things through.

She forced in a deep breath and tried to take stock. Cash was getting low, and she was afraid to use a card because that could be traced, right? And the man who'd attacked her—the monster who'd attacked her—was capable of anything.

She ran her hands over her arms, trying to still a shiver. She needed a plan. Soon.

No, she needed a plan right now. But what?

Work. A safe place. Those were the priorities. She needed to find work and lay low in a place as far off the beaten track as she could find.

A place like this.

She scanned the open, unfenced scrubland that no one seemed to claim as their own. What kind of teaching job would she ever find in the desert? Teaching was all she'd ever done, all she ever wanted to do.

But this wasn't about wanting. This was about survival. She could wait tables, clean floors, whatever it took.

She took one more look around and nodded, making up her mind. If nothing else, this place was fitting. It was open, endless, and brutally honest. Death might be hovering out on the fringes, but at least it couldn't sneak up on her here.

In her first decisive action since fleeing Pittsburgh, she slid back into the car, reached past the empty coffee cups on the passenger side floor, and dug out the map she hadn't checked since Texas. Where was she, exactly? Somewhere in Arizona—that much she knew. But where?

She glanced up at the scenery, down at the map, and up again. There'd been a town a couple of miles back, and that was as good a place to start as any. She gunned the engine to life and turned the car around. Twenty miles later, she was there: a tiny no-name town on the fringes of a slightly bigger, no-name town.

Heather checked into a motel that was only marginally less dusty than her car, slept thirty-six hours straight, then pulled herself together, one frayed thread at a time. A friendly waitress at a diner got her started with a phone book and a few names. It took dozens of calls, but within a couple of days, she found a tiny bungalow to rent on the edge of town and a job—a teaching job, even. A one-room schoolhouse on a lonely outpost of a ranch had a last-minute opening. In the interview, Heather rattled off her qualifications then rushed through the reason she'd left her job in Pennsylvania so abruptly.

"A stalker," she said. That was as close to the truth as she dared utter aloud.

It was enough—she got the job.

"It's only for two months," said Lana, the woman from the ranch. "Until our regular teacher comes back from emergency family leave."

"Two months is perfect." She'd catch her breath, earn a little cash, and then move on. Because sooner or later, the beast who hunted her would come looking. That much she knew.

# Chapter Two

The schoolhouse was a slanted old adobe, full of charm, if a little run-down, and the job was a bucking bronco, determined to pitch her off. But Heather was just as determined to hang on to this one scrap of sanity within her reach, even if it was the teaching challenge of her life. Eleven students, spread through all grades—from emerging readers to rowdy fifth graders. It took two bouncy weeks for her to convince that bronc to finally let her take the reins, but she did it. She found reserves of patience she didn't know she had, spent hours prepping lessons, and fell into bed exhausted each night. But she did it.

Once the kids settled into a new routine, everything got easier. Mornings were quieter, afternoons smoother. Right now, the kids were at their learning stations in pairs, working quietly while Heather went over essay writing with two third-graders.

A shriek drew her attention to the back of the schoolhouse, and she looked up then ducked on instinct. Something swept straight over her head, brushing her hair. Becky was screaming; Timmy was pointing. The room erupted into noise as the other kids joined in with high-pitched squeals that resounded off the walls.

"A bat! A bat!"

It made another pass, and Heather swiped the air over her head.

"Miss Luth! Miss Luth! A bat!"

She followed the silky black form until it perched on a high shelf. A tiny, pink tongue darted out and lapped at the air between them. She could swear its beady eyes were studying her. Something about the bat seemed...evil. She held back

5

a shudder and forced herself into action. "Timmy, get me a towel!"

For once, Timmy did as he was told. Heather approached the bat, towel in hand, kids cheering her on.

"Get it, Miss Luth! Get it!"

"Be careful, Miss Luth!"

Telling herself it was only a bat—one little bat—she lunged, but the bat was a step ahead, weaving and diving around the classroom. The noise level surged to a new peak, like a boxing arena at the first sight of blood.

"Everything okay?" A voice came from the doorway, completely unperturbed. It was soothing, like the sound of waves over a smooth, sandy shore. The voice warmed her from the inside even before she spun and spotted the newcomer.

"Cody! Cody!" the children cried.

Heather's stomach did a flip. It was him. The one she'd noticed around the ranch. The one she couldn't *not* notice.

The ranch seemed to be a breeding ground for gorgeous men, but this one was in a class of his own. Lean, blond, relaxed. Most of the others came in the strong-but-silent, earthy category, but this one should be bobbing on a surfboard, wiping salt water out of his eyes. He seemed in no hurry whatsoever, as if today was just another great day of many.

The kids whipped themselves into a new frenzy, pointing at the bat, high on another shelf.

"Cody! A bat! A bat!" Timmy jumped up and down on his desk, and a panicked Becky threw herself into the man's arms. He scooped her up and patted her back while Timmy shouted. "I saw it first! I saw it first!"

"Timmy, sit down!" Heather shot him her best teacher look.

Cody whispered to Becky, bringing a smile back to her face. Then he pointed at Timmy, eyes sparkling with mischief. "Do I know you?"

That voice could soothe a thousand wailing babies. She wanted to wrap it around her like a blanket.

"Cody! It's me, Timmy!"

He looked at the boy then right into Heather's eyes. Her heart skipped a beat. "I swear I don't know this child."

"Cody!" Timmy protested.

The man tousled Timmy's hair and lowered Becky back to her seat. Then he stepped up to Heather, eyes utterly, unfailingly devoted to hers. She caught a breath and held it. He'd never been this close before. Never done anything but wave a friendly hello from across the way. She'd had to force herself away every time because the urge to stop and talk— to look, to get closer, maybe even to touch—was damn near impossible to resist.

Now he was inches away. Big, broad—but not too much of either. Just right. The nick in one ear was the only part of him that wasn't perfect. She caught his scent, and it was an ocean breeze gone walkabout in the desert.

She gave herself an inner slap. No, no, no! Men were not to be trusted. Not ever again.

*Not even this one?* a small voice in her cried.

*Especially not this one!* came the slamming reply.

"Cody, get the bat!" the kids urged. "Get it! Get it!" Pandemonium once again.

A second voice boomed into the doorway, deep and gravelly. "What the hell is going on here?"

Without thinking, Heather wheeled, slammed her hands onto her hips, and shot out a reply. "Watch your language! This is a school!" For a moment, she felt like her old self—in command, not only of the students but herself. The Heather from before the nightmare.

When the second man stepped in, the air pressure in the room immediately rose, as if a storm system were squeezing itself through the doorway. Scampering feet pounded the wooden floorboards as kids rushed back to their seats and stood stiffly at attention. She could swear everyone was holding their breath—including the bat.

The man's piercing eyes glowed with anger. The old Heather might have stood her ground, but the Heather she'd become wavered and took a step back. She might have melted

7

onto the floor, mortified, if Cody hadn't stepped between them, practically growling.

Her shoulders slumped. Oh God, the second man was the ranch boss. She'd lose her job. She'd be thrown out. She'd—

"Don't mind my brother," Cody said softly.

That tenor was magic, sending a warm, secure rush her way. Heather straightened slightly and looked from Cody to the other one. Ty, that was his name. Were they really brothers? One was a thundercloud; the other, pure sunshine. As opposite as opposites can be.

Before she knew it, Ty whisked the towel out of her hands and stepped toward the bat. He must have fixed it with that laser of a gaze because the bat submitted without so much as lifting a wing. When Ty scooped it up and stepped outside, moving quickly down the flagstone path, the whole room exhaled.

Heather leaned against the wall, suddenly drained. "Five minute break, kids." They broke into gleeful cries and ran out to the playground, leaving Heather and Cody alone.

"My brother does have a soft spot, you know." Cody grinned. "It comes out every second year or so."

Definitely opposites, those two. She'd take this one in an instant and worship him like the sun.

His eyes were studying the blackboard, reading the words. "My dream home?" He grinned like Huck Finn, but all grown up. Very grown up.

She would bet anything he'd been like Timmy as a kid. Sweet, energetic, mischievous. And now, sweet, studly, and mischievous. She'd give anything to make like Becky and hide herself against that chest.

Heather cleared her throat. "Geometry. They have to find shapes in the house, and then draw their own dream homes."

"And this one is yours?" He nodded to the board.

The U-shaped ranch she'd been kidding herself about for years? She shrugged the notion away. "Nah. Just an example."

He chuckled. "Right."

God, that smile could make her forget everything. Like the fact that she'd sworn off men. Like the fact that she had eleven rambunctious kids to supervise instead of standing there, letting goose bumps tickle her skin.

Like the fact that the last man she'd let this close nearly killed her.

But with those sparkling blue eyes caressing hers, she just might forget.

"Cody!" Ty growled from outside, breaking whatever spell had wafted in with the wind.

"Gotta go," Cody sighed. He stood looking at her for a long, mournful minute—a kid watching the ice cream truck pull away before he got a scoop. "Gotta go," he repeated, eyes sliding shut. Seemed to Heather he'd aimed that whisper at himself.

And then he was gone, leaving the room emptier than it had ever felt before.

# Chapter Three

A hummingbird whizzed past, and Cody followed its cue, hurrying to catch up to his brother while trying not to let the visions dancing in his head trickle out. If Ty caught him thinking those thoughts...

But the visions persisted. Visions of a willowy woman with champagne-colored hair swirled in a bun. He dreamed of undoing that bun, finding out just how long and silky her hair was. Her eyes were as green as an Appalachian forest and just as haunted. She was tall, too. One little dip of his chin and they'd be kissing. He and the woman who stood up to his brother like an Amazon defending her turf. She only wavered when some memory jumped out and got the better of her. Cody wondered what it was, and what force had steered this human to his part of the continent.

*Destiny*, came a faint murmur, a whisper on the wind. Faint as it was, the sound still managed to hammer Cody's soul. His heart was pounding like he'd just run the length of the desert, searching for his mate.

Now why did that image come to him? That had been his brother, the closet romantic, holding out for years after a tiny hint of true love. Of Lana, his destined mate. Anyone who ever doubted destiny could look at those two and see proof.

Except Cody... Well, he wasn't Ty. On the rare occasion that destiny came knocking at the ranch, it brushed straight past him. Others might claim to have heard a call, but Cody? Nothing. Nada. The silent treatment.

Well, there was a message in that, too. That the second son of the ruling alpha wasn't destined for much. That, or he was captain of his own destiny and could damn well steer his own course. Cody didn't know which option unsettled him more.

He only knew that this stranger had stirred him like no woman before. He couldn't get her out of his mind. Before he'd even seen Heather, her presence had drawn him toward the schoolhouse he normally avoided. He found himself haunting the place, almost wishing he could take his old seat in the back and follow along. Hell, for her, he'd sit in the front. Raise his hand for every question and cry *Me! Me! Me!*

For reasons he couldn't understand, though, he'd been avoiding meeting her face-to-face—until now.

She was like no schoolteacher he'd ever met. Her legs belonged on a fashion runway—no, he decided, sportier than that. More like on a volleyball court. Her eyes were a green he'd never seen in the desert. And the toned arms stretching out from that sleeveless sundress, well, those belonged around him. He sniffed long and hard, savoring her scent like the last bloom of the century plant. Except this one came with a hint of strawberry. He did it again now: sniffed.

*Mine!* his wolf growled.

That's what scared him. His wolf had never claimed a woman before. Usually, the beast sampled anything on offer and quickly moved on, favoring quantity over quality when it came to the opposite sex. Over the last two weeks, though, his wolf had suddenly developed an opinion, and it was all about Heather.

Only her.

All the time.

*Mine!*

But what the hell did a wolf know?

Cody wasn't meant to settle down. Cody wasn't the one called by destiny. And he certainly didn't deserve a woman like her. She was so spirited. So together. So...fresh. But just because he got a rush around Heather, just because he spent day and night wondering about her, didn't mean he was in love. No, sir.

The wind taunted him all the way across the ranch.

Ty, the lucky bastard, had no such concerns. The man was happily mated and the father of an eighteen-month-old he adored. Ty didn't have to worry about finding his destiny; it had already found him.

Right now, he was intent on the bat, flipping back the towel for a closer look. Cody leaned in, too. They both knew that there were bats and there were... Well, call them bad bats, even if the latter hadn't been spotted in Arizona for decades. Cody studied the creature's eyes, the quivering tongue. It looked so fragile in his brother's big hand, yet somehow menacing, too.

"A scout?" Cody asked, keeping his voice low. Why, he wasn't sure. They were far enough away from the schoolhouse now, and Heather had turned the music on, anyway.

She'd danced through his senses, one after another, ever since she first arrived. It started with music—the notes had drawn him in on the very first day. He'd overheard her explaining the rules to the kids: they had to keep their voices down during independent work time, quiet enough for everyone to be able to hear the music. Good trick, that. She played classical stuff that no one on the ranch listened to—Beethoven, maybe Mozart, what did he know? It was sweet and calming, though, just like the sight of her. Cody sometimes stopped by just to listen, to know she was close.

Then it was scent, followed by sight, and now, Jesus, his fingers itched to touch her, to feel the silk of her hair, the smooth of her skin.

Ty tipped his head left, then right, still examining the bat. "Hard to say." They hadn't had vampires around here for a long time. Not the kind that made trouble, at least. But old fears ran deep. Ty wrapped the bat in the towel, careful not to crush it. Yet. "Dad wanted to see us. We'll show it to him."

Crap. Cody's day had started so well. He'd finally found an excuse to talk to Heather, finally got her to smile. Now everything was sure to go to hell.

*Coming?* Ty's voice invaded his mind. Siblings and pack-mates shared a close bond that enabled that form of communication. Some voices were weaker than others, but Ty's always came booming in, loud and clear.

*Coming, coming.* Cody let his feet shuffle along. Whatever their father wanted, it couldn't be good.

"Hi, Cody!" came a perky voice. Beth waved from the library porch, wearing a hopeful grin that harbored an open invitation.

He gave a neutral wave, ducked his chin, and hurried on. No use raising anyone's hopes.

"Hey, Cody," came a low, sultry call. His head swiveled left. Audrey stood there, leaning way over in a scooped top that displayed the bountiful goods on offer.

"Hi," he murmured, walking faster. He let a minute tick by before turning to Ty. "Do you miss that?"

"Not one bit." Ty shook his head.

"Not ever?"

"Never." Ty's voice left no room for doubt. Cody could see it on him anyway. These days, his brother positively glowed with happiness. It was as if Ty had found a whole new source of energy and was radiating it. Inexplicably, Cody found himself wondering what it was about having a child and a mate that was so satisfying. Wondering if he would ever find out for himself.

"Don't you get sick of it?" Ty asked.

Sick of the girls hitting on him all the time? Cody hesitated. Would his brother laugh if he said the truth? That he was tired of playing a role, tired of a different girl every week? Things had only gotten worse since Ty had mated with Lana, leaving Cody as most eligible bachelor on the ranch. For a time, he'd enjoyed himself. But now, it grated more than anything else.

Was he tired of loose, empty liaisons? Yes. Sick and tired.

"I love it," he said.

Ty snorted.

"Cody!" Audrey swept closer. The woman was hell in high heels. She raced up, staged a theatrical wobble, and launched herself right into his arms, making sure to heave her hefty rack into his chest.

If only she hadn't, because Cody bumped Ty, jarring him enough to shake the bat free. It circled once, twice, and flapped away. "Crap," Cody muttered.

Ty launched his curses directly into Cody's brain, along with everything he'd like to do to Audrey. Starting with throttling her with the lacy red bra advertising itself under her top.

"Oh, I'm sorry!" Audrey purred, fondling Cody's neck. "Was it important?"

*We'll never fucking know, will we?* Ty stomped off.

"Gotta go!" Cody said, peeling himself free. But he'd escaped the frying pan only to jump into the fire because the council house, where his father held court, was coming up next.

Getting there meant hurrying past two more packmates, both with issues to raise—real issues this time. Bryant had a question about the irrigation schedule, while Zack was reporting on fence damage. That was the thing: everyone came to Cody first. His father and Ty were both short on temper and patience. They kept the ranch running, but it was Cody and his sister Tina who kept it running smoothly. They were the approachable ones, the ones who convinced others with a smile and not a frown.

Cody exchanged a few quick words with each of the men then hurried into the council house.

"Ty," his father greeted his older son with his usual note of pride. The son he'd practically named after himself: Tyrone the father, Tyrell, the son. "Cody," he added in afterthought.

Cody tucked his lips together and kept still, except for a nod to his sister Tina, sitting to his father's right. She did her best to balance the old grouch out with a soft touch, as impossible as the task was. Ty and Tina were the spitting image of their father, dark and intense. Cody, he was different, in every way.

"Kyle called." As usual, his father launched right into business. The aspects of it that he still covered, that is. He'd gradually been handing duties over to his offspring, mainly playing the role of elder statesman—meaning he could meddle whenever he damn well pleased.

Cody and Ty exchanged glances. Kyle rarely had good news. A pack member who lived on the periphery of the ranch,

Kyle was also a state trooper. Their inside man.

"He was on about a series of murders in New Mexico," Tyrone continued with a dismissive flap of his hand.

Tina chimed in, outrage underpinning her voice. "Highway murders. Innocent women."

Tyrone gave an exaggerated sigh. "We should follow up. Kyle seems to think the killers might cross over to Arizona. We don't want trouble here."

If there was one thing shifters feared, it was discovery. Murder investigations brought outsiders, questions. In a word, trouble. Just because humans were the weaker species didn't mean they should be underestimated. Once upon a time, humans had hunted shifters to the brink of extinction. These days, Cody's kind had been relegated to the realm of myths, giving today's packs a measure of peace—as long as they remained incognito.

"I'll go," Cody said, eager for his chance.

Ty nodded. "Cody will take care of it."

He stood extra tall as his father's eyes raked his frame. He'd love an assignment like this. But would his father entrust it to him?

That was the thing. Cody had gone years engineering a persona for himself. Cody the reckless. Cody the playboy. He was no fool; even at a young age, he'd seen the crushing expectations heaped on his older brother. He wanted none of that, so he'd been sure to goof up frequently enough to keep expectations suitably low. And for a long time, the strategy worked.

The problem was, he was getting a little tired of acting his own role. But he was so good at it now, he was typecast. Didn't matter that he was ready to handle responsibility. Didn't matter that he'd earned number three rank in the pack on his own merits. His father saw only the little boy. This was a chance, maybe *the* chance, to prove himself.

His father eyed him skeptically.

"I can do it," Cody insisted.

Their father looked to Ty instead. Lucky for Cody, his brother's hands shot up. "I've got enough to do here. Lana's got a stack of work, too, and Tana's got a cold."

Cody hid a smile at Ty's unabashed words. So what if their father was scowling again? Ty was committed to playing an active role in his child's upbringing and being a good mate—unlike their father in his time. Ty might be the spitting image of their father, but he was a totally different man. A good man.

Cody's eyes drifted to his own feet. What would his own legacy be?

An image of Heather formed, so real and close it nearly knocked him off his feet. Those green eyes, smiling right into his, showing him just how good the future could be. Telling him how much more he could be. He didn't have to be the overlooked son of a powerful alpha. He could be—

And then it hit him. Whatever he might become, it would have to be without her. Because the son of the alpha could never, ever take a human mate. He was supposed to continue the shifter bloodline by claiming one of their own. Everyone knew it. Some other wolfpacks tolerated human mates, but Twin Moon was an old-fashioned kind of place, and humans were strictly forbidden—and doubly forbidden to the alpha's son.

His inner wolf let out a low, continuous growl at the thought, throwing crazy messages at the human half of his mind. Like fighting for Heather. Claiming her. Taking her as his mate—

Cody winced at a burning sensation on his ear, and then looked up to see his brother hitting him with one of his piercing looks. A look that said, *Whatever you're thinking about, it better not be her.*

"Cody can do it," Tina said, surprising him with the conviction in her words. "He can work with Kyle to stop the killer before another innocent victim dies, and before any reporters or investigators bring trouble."

They all knew what kind of trouble Tina meant. The pack kept a low profile for a good reason—their own survival.

He pushed the image of Heather out of his mind and looked his father in the eye, willing the words to fall from those skeptical lips. A long, uncertain pause followed. Outside, a wood-pecker hammered, then listened to its own echo, and a pick-up rattled past, kicking up a plume of dust. Seconds creaked by.

Finally, Tyrone nodded. "Cody, take care of it."

Music to his ears.

*Just watch you don't fuck it up,* Ty grunted.

Ah, Ty—helpful as ever.

Their father flapped his hand, dismissing them. Cody forced himself to walk to his truck at a measured pace. He fired it up and pointed it for the ranch gate, ready to roll, then paused abruptly. This murder case was unlikely to be resolved quickly. He might be tied up for weeks, pulling long hours away from the ranch.

Away from Heather. His heart plummeted.

Though it was probably for the best. He couldn't afford to let himself get distracted now. Not with just another fling—with a human, of all things.

*Fling?* His wolf roared so fiercely, so offended, that the truck swerved. *Mine! Mate!*

# Chapter Four

Heather heard the clock tick but didn't look up. It was late, too late, to still be at work, especially three weeks into the job when things should have tapered off. But teaching six grade levels a day meant a mountain of preparation. That and she'd sworn off Friday nights. Sworn off men, too, since the time when bad went to worse and worse became a nightmare.

The ghost of her reflection haunted her laptop screen, pale and unearthly. She'd changed so much, looking fragile, fearful, and hunched. An old spinster at age twenty-seven. The only place Heather felt like her old self was in school. Maybe that's why she put in the extra hours. What happened to the confident woman who didn't let herself get pushed around?

Simple, Heather reminded herself. That woman had nearly gotten herself killed. That woman's judgment couldn't be trusted. Never again.

Especially now that she was battling an inexplicable pull toward a man she barely knew. Cody. The man had hijacked her thoughts and refused to negotiate a release. Ever since he'd stopped by to deal with the bat, it was all she could do to draw a breath without it having something to do with him. Over the past week, he'd been turning up at the schoolhouse almost daily, just as she was wrapping things up. He'd been spending a lot of time off the ranch on some project, but even so, he'd magically appear, loping toward her like a joyous puppy who'd just slipped his leash.

"Hiya!"

It was getting so that Heather didn't even need to look up to know who it would be.

19

"Hey," she would call back, trying to keep the jitter out of her voice.

"Looks like you're going my way." He'd smile and fall in step with her.

"Looks like." She would nod, trying not to show her delight. She could get drunk just from being this close.

They'd walk side by side, and Heather would slow her step to drag out the simple pleasure of his company.

"Can I carry something for you?" That had become part of the routine, too. And every single time, his smooth voice rose in hope.

All she had was an empty lunch bag and a work bag with her laptop and a notebook inside; not exactly a heavy load. But she'd swing the work bag off her shoulder and offer it to him all the same. On the first day, he'd goaded her all the way to the parking lot before she gave it up. Now she handed it over without argument, finding a strange kind of satisfaction in having a man want to do something for her, even if she didn't need it. Just because.

They'd walk and chat, and that became the highlight of her day. Like yesterday, when his proximity made her warm, tingly, and safer than she'd felt in what seemed like a lifetime.

"So, what's your next project in the schoolhouse?" he asked. The man was always so relaxed, so assured. She wished just a tiny bit of that could rub off on her. But then she'd get to wishing for a lot more than a fleeting touch, and that inner voice of warning would strike.

*Watch out! You can't trust him! Can't trust anyone!*

She knew she should hold back, but it was impossible. The man could charm the gold out of Fort Knox just on the force of his grin. A grin that stirred up a warm, thick pulsing in her veins.

"Well, I'd set up a reading nook if I could."

"A reading nook?" He arched an eyebrow. "I'm picturing leather straps. Hard chairs. Instruments of torture."

That Cody hadn't enjoyed his school days, she'd already guessed. He had probably been the type with too much energy to sit still, too much humor to harness.

"No, all a reading station needs is a couple of beanbags and a cozy rug."

"Cozy, huh?" He gave an impish grin.

Heather decided not to acknowledge the flame that lit inside her. "And it has to have a theme," she added, feeling hopelessly girlish as the words came out. The man exuded so much testosterone, instinct had her counterbalancing him.

"A theme," he echoed, skepticism in his voice.

"I was thinking an underwater theme. A blue rug, like the sea..." *Like your eyes*, though she left that part out. "I'd put the books in a box made to look like a treasure chest, and paint the wall in an underwater scene."

"Like what, an octopus holding eight books?" A smile played at the corners of his lips. Either he was making mental notes or kidding her. Hard to tell which.

She nodded, gulping away images of a bare-chested Cody entering the schoolhouse with four cans of paint in one hand— because hands as broad as his were capable of great feats—and a brush in the other. A little smudge of blue on his cheek, a line of yellow on his pecs.

Her heart beat just a little faster. "An octopus reading eight books at once. Great idea."

He was delighted, she could tell, and her heart squished just a little more. Hadn't anyone ever praised his ideas before?

Every day it went something like that, the two of them walking and grinning like fools. He'd drop her off at the car and wouldn't turn away until she was around the bend. She knew because she watched him, too, and the rubber band tugging her toward him grew harder to resist on each successive day.

But she had to resist. Even if he meant her no harm, she was just passing through Arizona on her way to... somewhere. Some place to hide and survive.

So it was probably a good thing that some days, he didn't turn up at all. Like today, when not even an hour of hopeful glances or anxious finger-tapping could conjure him out of thin air.

She sighed and looked out the window. Outside, the sun had just slipped below the western hills, bleeding red and orange across the sky. The colors scribbled a reminder of what she'd been told when she first took the job. *Avoid the dirt road after dark.* A polite hint, she figured, to get off ranch property by nightfall. She wasn't sure why, but she didn't want to step on any toes. The job meant too much to her.

Never mind that back in town, rumors flew. The ranch harbored some kind of cult, people said. The way the ranch folk sequestered themselves, the way they kept outsiders at arm's length... It was a cult, for sure.

Heather had long since dismissed the rumors. She hadn't seen any sign of a cult, only nice, hard-working people. If anything was unusual on the ranch, it was how neighborly everyone was, in an old-fashioned kind of way. She felt perfectly at ease in this haven from the outside world. In fact, it was an effort to drag herself away.

But day was tipping into night in that uncertain hour when the desert awoke from its siesta, and it was time to go. Heather hastened to collect her things then stood and turned off the lights. Outside, the first stars were twinkling, asking why she had to go. Every time she headed out, she got this melancholy feeling. As if home was here and not in town.

Soon, too soon, Heather was in the central courtyard where her car was parked. She sucked in a deep breath and took in the timeless atmosphere for the hundredth time. The ranch brand hung swinging over the entry gate: two circles, overlapping by one third. Century-old cottonwoods arched overhead, wise and aloof. False-fronted buildings with wooden boardwalks lined up like a Wild West film set, right down to the palomino swinging its tail beside a hitching post. In spring, they said, the trees bloomed with cottony fluff that blanketed the place like snow. It ached, knowing she couldn't stay long enough to see the seasons change in this fascinating place.

The first notes of a guitar drifted from the barn, along with a babble of voices. Light glowed from within the flung-back doors, and before she knew it, Heather's feet carried her closer. From the looks of it, a dance was just getting underway. Colored lights were strung overhead, and a three-man band made up of a couple of ranch hands launched into a sweet country ballad. It was an old-time, open-air dance where kids ducked between the trees and giggled at dancing couples, young and old. The music was soft, the laughter hearty. Heather found herself lingering, watching. Wishing.

To belong. Somewhere.

Well, she might not belong here, but if she walked very slowly, she could at least watch. Her eyes scanned the faces and immediately picked out Cody, standing with two gray-haired women, his eyes fixed on the dance floor. His brother, the thundercloud, was dancing with Lana, the woman who had interviewed Heather for the job. The two of them were cheek to cheek, hip to hip, swaying slowly to their own beat. A molasses beat, Heather thought. Lana whispered something that made Ty smile then nuzzle her ear. A toddler ran over; Ty scooped his daughter up, snuggled her close, and went right on dancing, the three of them tight as a knot.

A few steps away, another tall man spun his lithe partner into a turn, and then pulled her back in tight, as if even that had been too far apart for his liking. Something inside Heather ached just watching them. It must be Zack and his partner Rae. The school kids were full of crazy stories about those two, none of which Heather believed. Hunts? Bows and arrows? Tracking by smell? The only part she believed was the part about Zack's cool Harley.

Her focus slow-zoomed back to Cody. A wistful look flashed across his face before he went back to easygoing Cody—the one who looked like he'd just sauntered over from some great waves at the beach. Heather held her breath when a pretty brunette stepped up to him. She exhaled when the woman retreated, looking miffed. Another wasn't far behind. The bleached blond with big hair and big boobs. Heather prepared to turn away so she wouldn't have to watch Cody dance with her. Because the man who met her at the schoolhouse door and carried her school bag wasn't supposed to dance with anyone else.

But he didn't. He turned each and every one of them away. Who was he waiting for, wishing for?

Then Heather saw who. The dark-haired beauty he was smiling at now, the one crooking a finger to draw him out on the dance floor. Cody went without hesitation and swept her into his arms. Every turn, every contact they exchanged made Heather wince.

She turned away quickly and brushed a hand across her cheek, pretending that wasn't a tear she caught. Not like she wanted a man, anyway. Especially one who could break so many hearts—or one heart, over and over. Anyway, hadn't it been a beautiful Friday night like this that had started so well and ended so badly, not too long ago?

She slammed a door on those memories. She was here now, thousands of miles from the East Coast. Safe. For now, anyway.

Her car wasn't far now, a timid dwarf between two dusty trucks. She walked slowly, face to the stars—so many more than she'd ever seen back East. Behind her, the music was winding down as one song gave way to another. She opened the creaky back door of her hatchback and threw in her bag, then made for the front, determined to quit this place and thoughts of a man who kindled impossible desires.

A spark beyond the front bumper captivated her attention, though, and she lingered just a minute longer. A tiny flash, then another. Fireflies were dancing, lighting up the night. Another few minutes passed as she watched them play peeka-boo.

"Hiya."

If it had been any other voice, Heather would have jumped out of her skin. But it was that honeydew tenor that lubricated her soul. Cody.

She turned to find him standing by the neighboring truck, and her heart started up that pathetic pitter-patter pattern it did every time he came near.

"I was kind of hoping..." he started, looking suddenly wistful. "You're not leaving already, are you?"

The voice of the spinster croaked inside. *Don't trust him! Don't trust anyone!*

Her tight shoulders, though, immediately relaxed. Cody felt like a long-lost friend. One she had missed terribly, all these years.

24

# Chapter Five

Cody's gaze flicked to the fireflies in the bush, and she swore his eyes danced in the same way. "We used to count them when we were little," he chuckled. "Well, we tried."

Heather tried it, just to silence the voice inside. One, two. Three. Four? Hard to tell, the way they disappeared from one place and reappeared in another. She noticed Cody slipping closer then noticed something else. That Cody was the only man who could do that without setting off a galloping fear. Ever since she'd been attacked, a man stepping into line at the grocery store behind her was enough to make her flinch. But Cody... the closer, the better.

*Get away! Just keep him in your dreams. Nice dreams. Intimate dreams, where he'll always be gentle and kind. Don't let him close!*

But he was close. Closer now. Power glinted off him like the sun off the ocean—power and something more. Not greed, not lust. Just... a yearning. That was it.

Heather searched for something, anything to say. "Guess I better go." She spoke the words, but her limbs refused to move. Not when he stood so near.

"What's the rush? Got a date?" With his fair hair backlit by party lights, he looked like the son of Apollo and not a mere mortal.

Heather shook her head. "No rush." Definitely no date. But didn't he have one—the dark-haired beauty? "You're a good dancer," she blurted as the image swung through her mind.

"Only with my sister. With anyone else, I've got two left feet."

His sister? Heather's mind pulled up the image of the woman. "That's your sister?"

"My half sister, Tina. You remember Ty?"

The thundercloud? "Sure."

"He and Tina came first. Then my father got together with my mother and had me and my little sister, Carly."

Now it made sense. His dark-haired dance partner did resemble Ty, and when Heather replayed the scene, she realized they'd danced loose and light. Nothing like the intimacy between Ty and Lana. She exhaled. "Half sister, huh?"

Cody cracked a smile. "Doesn't mean she's only half bossy to her poor, innocent little brother."

"Innocent?" Little? Sweet, sensual, yes. But not innocent. And nowhere near little.

The golden smile of a guilty man flashed. "Absolutely innocent."

"Why do I doubt that?" she managed.

"I don't know. Why?"

"Oh, just because." *Because I see the laughter in your eyes. Because of the way you hide behind your smile. Because that nick in your ear tells a different story.*

She'd been watching him the past few days. At first, she fell for that happy-go-lucky cowboy persona. But every so often, she'd catch his mask slipping, as it had when he watched his brother dance. Underneath, Cody's eyes flashed with fierce determination—to do what, she couldn't tell. Then he'd catch himself and paste the smile back on. How often had she seen that in her students? Once a child assumed a role—class clown, science nerd, beauty queen, whatever—it was hard to let it go.

Cody. Little boy, lost and lonely, or grown man, tough and unassailable? He hadn't quite found his balance between the two.

Right now, the mask was firmly in place. "I was a very good boy!" He winked. "If you leave out the time with the skunk and the glue on the chair..."

She knew the type exactly. And how hard it was to break out that self-imposed persona. She turned to the car. "I really should get moving."

"No dancing?"

Heather shrugged. Not invited. She was an outsider here, just as she'd been everywhere else.

"What's the hurry?"

"They said I shouldn't stay after dark."

His voice dropped, face earnest. "One dance before you go?"

She tilted her head at him. "I thought you had two left feet."

A grin, small but sincere. She wanted to reach out and grab hold of him—the real Cody, now.

"Let me prove it." The way his words hit the air made Heather wonder what else he had to prove.

He put his hand out, and the gesture brought her to a different place, a different night. The night she nearly died. For a moment, all her muscles threatened to shut down. Heather swallowed the scream, blinking the panic away.

His eyes narrowed on hers, and she caught her breath. Unlike the eyes of that terrifying night, these were blue, tinged with gold. Safe eyes.

"Everything okay?" His voice was soft, coaxing her back from the edge of a cliff. Heather nodded robotically. She could do this.

"I'm fine." Right. Now she was the one wearing a mask.

Slowly, carefully, like a man handling a spooked filly, Cody led her to the small space between her front bumper and a hitching post. His hands were callused and strong. Comforting, even.

The spinster's voice was back in Heather's head. *Not so close!* But only her ears got the message; the rest of her was melting fast.

Cody stepped into a slow dance. Not too close, not too tight, just...nice. They fit together just right, her chin just over his shoulder, his arm around the curve of her waist.

*Get away! Get home!*

Home? Home felt like right here.

Heather promised herself she wouldn't get carried away. She'd head home soon. She'd—

Snuggle her cheek against his? The salty scent of the sea was there, so crisp and fresh she knew it wasn't just cologne. Music drifted past, maybe on the same magical ether that made her feet so light. Her head felt light, too. The man who had turned down all of those women wanted to dance with her.

Her skin was tingling. "You definitely don't have two left feet," she murmured. He kept his nose to her hair. God, that felt good.

"The left foot is mine. The right foot is yours." His voice was husky; his heart tapped an oath for every word. "We're made for each other, you and me."

The warning voice, meanwhile, cried from a distant and rapidly sinking ship. *Don't trust anyone...*

Then he stopped dancing and his eyes were on her lips, and it was impossible to heed anything but the call to meet him halfway. He leaned in just as she rocked forward on her toes, holding her breath as they kissed.

It was a meltdown kiss, long and light. So perfect that she had to close her eyes to take it all in.

His lips were soft. Silky. Innocent. Maybe the man hadn't been bullshitting her, after all. Because kissing Cody was like riding a puffy white cloud through a gorgeous summer sky. She leaned in, wanting more. His lips shaped tiny letters over hers, starting with a gentle B, and then slowly moving on to an M that massaged her mouth. Then his lips opened, forming vowels—little A's and O's that tasted like heaven. That kiss stretched on and on, and she didn't want the alphabet to ever run out. In the end, it was Cody who broke it off slowly, puckering so that they would only part at the last possible moment.

If it hadn't been him there with his eyes closed, drinking in that kiss, it would have been her.

Her heart thumped, about to lean in for a second round, but a bat fluttered past, swooshing right over their heads.

They broke apart to let it pass, and to Heather, the separation hurt. It actually hurt.

So did reality: the fact that she should have been on the road by now. That this could never be.

"I have to go," she whispered.

His face flickered, a signal that the mask was back. The cool bachelor, the jokester, was about to cover his tracks with a witty line. But no—he caught it and shot her a tight smile instead, one tinged with regret. "See you soon?"

Heather sucked in a deep breath. It could never be soon enough. She nodded then slipped into the car and drove away, eyes more on the rearview mirror than the road ahead.

# Chapter Six

Fear and desire. Cody had never smelled one so close to the other. He replayed the encounter over and over, through the night and into the next day. He wanted more of that kiss. Wanted to do it again and again, soft and light until he'd kissed away that haunted look in her eyes.

Who did that to her? Who scared her right to the bone? Because even when she lit up at his kiss, she was afraid. The thought had his wolf straining at its bonds. He wanted to chase after her car and stay close. Keep her safe. Make her his.

*Mate! Don't let her go!*

It took a long and sweaty night for Cody to realize that it wasn't just his wolf claiming her; the man was howling for her now, too. It was all he could do not to rush out in search of her at the crack of dawn. But one dance would have to be enough—for now.

He had to figure things out first. Like if he was really sure.

*How can you not be sure?* the wolf growled.

Okay, maybe he was sure. But what did it matter if the pack would never accept her? And anyway, *she* had to be sure. And how the hell could he ever get past that step? It's not like he could just out and tell her.

*Heather, my wolf and I want you to be our mate. Let me bite you and make you mine forever.*

Jesus, it would sound like some kind of horror show to her. And he'd never be able to explain. What would he say?

*I promise it won't hurt, baby.*

Right. Like that would work, even if it were true. Mated wolves—male and female—all flashed sultry grins when they

31

talked about the mating bite. Like it was the highest of all highs. But even if it were true, she'd think he was nuts.

And really, what did he have to offer her?

*Undying love?* his wolf, suddenly a poet, filled in.

Like that would be enough. Bringing any human around to the idea of mating a shapeshifter would be hard enough. Bringing a frightened one—no matter how tough she pretended to be—would be even harder. He'd have to bide his time, give her space.

Except time was the enemy. Heather's teaching contract only lasted for a few more weeks. He had only that long to convince her to stay. To be his.

Only that long to convince the pack to accept a human. But Christ, that would take an eternity.

*Why wait?* his wolf murmured, low and angry. *We just take her now! They can't stop us after the mating bite.*

Cody pushed the beast back into its cage. That wasn't the right way to go about winning his mate. For now, he had to wait. In the meantime, he needed to support Kyle with the murder case, even with Heather's wild strawberry scent lingering in his nose.

He'd woken the morning after the kiss—Saturday—to the news that there'd been another highway murder, this time in Arizona. The killer was moving closer to pack territory. Cody drove three hours east in grim silence to where he'd meet Kyle. He tried listening to his usual radio station on the way but quickly flipped to a new channel. That lovestruck cowboy stuff was not what he needed to hear right now.

There, a classic road song. That was better.

He lasted all of thirty seconds, though, before flipping back to the crooning cowboy. *Waiting hearts and sharpened darts...* Junk, but somehow, it struck a chord in him.

Except he needed to keep his mind on the job and not the woman, so he turned it off again. But even that didn't keep her out of his mind—all the way across the state and into the parking lot of the Graham County morgue where his packmate was waiting.

He followed Kyle's heavy boots to the lower level of the building. Kyle flashed his badge, hammered down a corridor, and pushed through a pair of heavy metal doors.

"Officer Williams," the coroner greeted Kyle. Behind him, a body lay stretched on the examination table.

Cody shook his head, glancing at it. *Jesus.* He couldn't see her face, but she looked young. Too young to die such a violent death.

Kyle nodded. "Doctor Nguyen." He motioned toward Cody. "This is Officer Hawthorne of the Nevada Highway Patrol."

That was Cody's cover story, one backed up by a genuine-looking badge. Kyle's, on the other hand, was the real thing. He was one of the few pack members who worked a job in the human world—a job with fringe benefits as far as the pack was concerned. It never hurt to get a heads-up on crimes and investigations in the area, whether those involved shifters or not.

The coroner nodded without shaking hands and led them to the examination table.

She was the third murder victim in a series that had just extended from New Mexico into Arizona. Like the others, she'd been lured to the side of the highway then repeatedly slashed and left to die. So far, police had nothing. No prints, no witnesses, no leads.

Cody stepped up slowly, wishing he could somehow give this woman back her dignity. He could see her from the chest down, lying naked on cold steel, gashed in a dozen places. A shell without a soul.

"We have an ID on the victim," the coroner started. "Age twenty-six, no criminal record. No sign of drugs or alcohol. Roommates reported nothing suspicious when she left home."

Cody clenched a fist to keep his claws sheathed. God, he'd like to give the killer a taste of his own medicine.

The coroner went through his report in a monotone, detailing one gash after another. "Rough-edged blade, here, here, and here. But look closer," he said, pointing to a slash on the victim's abdomen.

Cody stepped forward, catching sight of her face. His hand splayed on the table to keep his knees from buckling at the sight of champagne-colored hair and startled green eyes trained lifelessly on the ceiling.

"What's the matter, Officer Hawthorne," Kyle goaded, "seen a ghost?"

Now that the first shock was past, Cody could see it wasn't Heather. But the resemblance was close. Too close. He shot a mental roar off to Kyle to put him in his place and took grim satisfaction in watching the man wobble at the unexpected force of it. Didn't hurt to remind the man who held rank here.

"This is the unusual part," the coroner explained, oblivious to his audience. "A puncture wound, underneath."

Cody froze. It was a worst-case scenario, if it was what he suspected. He forced a neutral expression over his face as he listened to the coroner go on.

"Most of the wounds are too deep and rough to ascertain if there are more puncture marks. But this one bears a trace."

Cody followed Kyle's eyes to the victim's neck. "Nowhere else?" Kyle asked, voice a forced calm. His fingers scraped through his short, spiky hair.

"Nowhere," the coroner said and continued with his report. "Evidence of rape..." His flat monotone only made the word uglier.

Cody slipped behind Kyle to lean in over the woman's neck. He sniffed, close. Nothing but the last traces of a cheap perfume mixed with the acrid smell of fear. No trace of what he was looking for. He shook his head at Kyle.

"Whoever bled her, he was a thorough son of a bitch," the coroner added. "Bled her completely dry. Not à drop left."

Kyle shot Cody a meaningful look. *Are you thinking what I'm thinking?*

Cody wished he didn't. But he nodded. *Vampire.*

∞∞∞∞

An examination of the crime scene, out on a remote stretch of highway, affirmed their fears. The ashy scent of vampire was all over the victim's car. To Cody, they all smelled the same. Like death. Like evil. Something that was there, but not there, like the last trace of ammonia overpowering the stink of something unclean. But even keen wolf noses couldn't track them. Vampires only left a scent when they fed. As far as a trail was concerned, the killers had vanished into thin air.

"Vampires," Kyle muttered on the long drive east. They were headed over the state border to confer with investigators working on the previous murders. "From New Mexico? Texas?"

Cody didn't care where they came from. He wanted them dead.

"Must have been a couple of them, feeding on her at once," Kyle speculated.

Cody sucked in a breath to fight the bitter taste in his mouth. A lone vampire could be a handful, even for a wolf. His father still bore the scars from a fight with a vampire he'd only barely overcome, long before Cody's birth. Vampires were quick and very, very hard to kill. A fight with more than one vampire promised a high body count on both sides.

"Then they covered up by slashing her," Kyle finished.

A long pause filled the car while their imaginations filled in the rest.

"Think Zack and Rae could track them?" Kyle asked.

Cody immediately shook his head. Zack was the pack's best tracker and Rae, a master hunter, but even they wouldn't be of any help with this kind of trail. "Like Zack would let his mate get anywhere near vampires," he added with a snort. As if any good mate would allow that.

The thought cued an image of Heather, and his pulse jumped with the urge to protect. He checked his watch, calculating the hours since he'd last seen her. Already much too long. If this threat of vampires hadn't pushed everything else aside, he could be with her now.

"When I get my claws on those blood suckers..." He left the threat hanging.

The investigators in New Mexico were just as baffled by the crimes, but hours of poring over maps and police records revealed nothing.

"Hell of a way to spend a Saturday night," one of the investigators said.

Or a Sunday morning, because Cody and Kyle ended up spending the night in New Mexico, following what turned out to be false leads. By the time they got back to Kyle's Arizona headquarters, it was late on Sunday. Another two hours of checking records also failed to turn up anything. Cody huffed into his coffee cup and tossed it aside.

"How do you do this all the time?"

"What?" Kyle raised an eyebrow.

"The deaths. The unsolved mysteries. The fucked-up shitheads responsible for them."

Kyle's eyes traveled along the office wall, landing no place in particular. His brow furrowed, and suddenly Cody wished he hadn't asked. Because his packmate's eyes showed pain then gritty determination. The man was a cop for a reason, even if he didn't reveal much about his past.

Kyle swallowed, and then pulled back into focus. "This is the hard part—waiting, thinking, messing with false leads. But catching the bastards—that feels good." He looked at Cody, his eyes burning with resolve. "We'll solve this case. I promise you that."

"We'll get the bastards, all right," Cody replied, thumping his tilted-back chair back to the floor.

At that moment, though, there was nothing to do but to call it a night. Cody headed to Kyle's place, where he planned to bunk for the night instead of driving all the way back to the ranch. The house—the old blacksmith's house, out on the far edge of Twin Moon territory—was as messy as Kyle's life had once been. But he'd gotten himself together remarkably well for a human inadvertently turned wolf in a messy biker brawl that included a rogue shifter. That the cop even survived his wounds was a small miracle. Only the strongest humans survived those kinds of wounds and became shifters.

Kyle joined Twin Moon pack shortly after recovering and slowly found his way into a new life. Still, it was obvious that the man had a long way to go before he was comfortable in his own skin—both skins, to be precise. He spent too much time on his own, staring off into space, studying the ghosts of his past. Or maybe he was dreaming of something forever out of reach. Whatever it was, the man seemed more empty shell than soul. The girls loved it, though. Kyle had that wounded warrior aura they just couldn't resist.

Cody threw his friend a sidelong look and wondered for the first time if he got tired of it, too. Tired of loose and empty hookups instead of... Instead of the steady rightness of a mate's company.

And off his mind went on another round of imagining something that couldn't be.

Cody brooded throughout their pizza dinner and the first half of the football game running on the TV, unable to shake the image of the dead woman's startled eyes. Eyes so much like Heather's. His legs twitched with the impulse to go check on the schoolhouse. Except Heather would be home today. His pulse jumped at the idea. He could track her down. She lived somewhere in town, didn't she?

Right. He'd show up unannounced and say... what exactly? *Hi, Heather. I needed to check that you're okay. I need to hold you close.*

Like that would get past her armor.

Or maybe a different tack. *I can't forget our kiss. Want about a million more like it.* The kiss echoed in his mouth now, taking the edge off the acid taste that still clung there after the morgue. *And, by the way, I want you to be my mate.* He could just imagine how well that would go over.

Cody tried shaking off the feeling. He shouldn't, couldn't think of Heather now.

Kyle pointed the remote at the TV. "Hey, Code." He hit mute but kept his eyes on the game.

"Yeah?"

"Want some advice?"

Cody worked his jaw from side to side. "No."

Silence filled the room until Kyle hit the sound button, flooding the space with cheers.

Cody let another tackle go down before giving in. "Okay, what?"

"Let it go for tonight. We need clear heads for tomorrow."

Cody shot Kyle a hard look, reminding him who beat whom in that fight they'd had shortly after Kyle joined the pack. It had been a hard-fought encounter, and even in defeat, Kyle had earned high standing in the pack.

Right now, though, Cody had to admit Kyle was right. He should clear his head. But how? The vampires were out there. Who knew who their next victim would be? And Heather... He just couldn't clear his mind of her. It was as if the part of his brain responsible for breathing had taken her on, too.

The wolf leaped to attention and started pacing. *Mate! Mine!*

No, no, no. He couldn't let himself get distracted. Not when so much was on the line.

His wolf growled disapproval just as something beeped. Kyle leaned over the side table. "Fax from Tina for you."

Cody sighed; his wolf whined. Tina probably had some errand for him to run tomorrow. More likely, an entire series of errands like hauling fertilizer and tracking down hard-to-find parts. She loved torturing her little brother like that.

When Cody read the fax though, he broke into a wide grin. *Need you to bring this to Heather,* Tina wrote. *Beth's library orders. Does Heather want to add anything before we put the order in tomorrow morning?* Below that, she'd jotted Heather's address. *P.S. Hope you don't mind.*

Nope. He didn't mind one bit.

But showing up at Heather's place unannounced with a sheaf of papers seemed a little lame, so Cody stopped by a store on the way. He wavered between the aisles, plagued by indecision. Wine seemed a little too forward. Beer, a little too crude. He settled on two pints of strawberries instead.

Thoughts of the murder case flitted away, replaced by images of her. A mile away from her address, his nostrils were already twitching. When Cody took the final turn down her quiet lane, he immediately recognized that late model orange VW of hers, so out of place here in the west. The car had seen better days and the tiny rental bungalow, too. But it was quiet out here on the edge of town, and she'd done her best to spruce things up with potted plants and a bird feeder. In them, he saw the color of hope, of determination to make a new start. Which only made him more curious. What brought her to Arizona, anyway?

*Destiny,* the desert whispered.

He sniffed. She was home, all right. Everything in him skipped and lurched, and Cody nearly laughed at himself. Other men came home sniffing for dinner; he came home sniffing for her.

Then he caught himself. Home wasn't here.

*She's here,* his wolf said. *Home.*

He locked the beast back into its cage and knocked, knuckles rapping beside a braid of garlic. Funny, most people hung strings of chili peppers on their doors. Heather was different. Different in so many fascinating ways. Cody knocked again and stepped back, prepping the words he'd been rehearsing all the way over. But the moment she opened the door, he froze. Not so much at the T-shirt and shorts she'd changed into as at her hair, finally let down. Light filtered through it, accenting every soft strand that went down nearly to her waist in long, golden waves. Gone was the teacher; before him was someone between girl and woman, innocent and sensual all at the same time. Like her scent—a light, fruity scent, as if she'd just stepped out of the shower in anticipation of his visit.

Her scent filled him and words vanished. Everything disappeared, replaced by a roar in his ears, a twitch in his veins.

*Mine!* screamed his wolf. *Make her mine!*

# Chapter Seven

A knock on the door on a Sunday night should have set off every alarm in Heather's body. It should have had her cowering, hoping that whoever it was, they'd please, please give up and go away.

Part of her did cower. But the other part was drawn forward—bold and unafraid. Reckless, even. As if her dog Buddy were there, one step ahead, tail wagging in eager anticipation of a trusted friend. That's what the night air was signaling now: friend, not foe.

Slowly, carefully, she turned the lock and cracked the door open, bracing to bash it closed, just in case.

It was him. Cody. More than a friend; her heart knew that already. Each time he walked her to her car, another section of her heart caved in. And two nights ago, that kiss had sent the rest crumbling. She could still taste him on her lips, still feel his hand on her hip. She'd been bumping into her own furniture, pouring tea into her cereal, watching the clock for some unknown appointment.

Now, standing before her, Cody's eyes sparkled gold behind the brown, like coins in an ancient well. In faded denim and a beige shirt, the man was all dry tones, but his hands cupped something succulent and red. Behind him, the desert was hushed, leaning in to eavesdrop.

They stood staring at each other for a minute, or maybe ten, bathed in silence except for the hum. It was very faint, like a power station radiating electricity, but it came from between them, out of thin air. Or maybe it was from the thirsty earth below, thrumming with the beat of a primal drum.

41

The lazy, lusty heat of it wrapped around Heather's legs and clambered up her frame. Soon she'd be engulfed with that thumping need. Did he feel it, too? She stood silent, wondering what it was that tore at her gut with a curt, urgent message: *Cody! Cody!* It might have been the call a hibernating bear gets to wake up or a flower to bloom. Every scrap of her was being pulled in his direction.

"Hi," he breathed. His voice, normally so smooth, had a bit of sandpaper in it tonight.

"Hi," she said, or at least mouthed it while her pulse hammered in her ears.

Warning bells sounded in her mind. *Don't trust him! Don't trust anyone!*

His lips parted as if to speak then closed again. She could taste the kiss forming on them as he took her in. Not the way some men did, appraising and crude. No, his gaze was gentle, sincere. Hopeful, too. But he was holding back, giving her the power to choreograph what happened next.

*Danger! Danger! You don't know what he will do!*

Heather shoved the spinster aside and swung the door wide. "Would you like to come in?"

Grinning like a boy offered a cookie jar and trying to remember his manners, Cody stepped over the threshold. "Tina asked me to give you this." He handed her a limp sheaf of papers. Meanwhile, all his focus—his hopes—were pinned to his other hand. The one that held out strawberries. Juicy. Sweet. Begging to be devoured.

Temptation, there for her to take or reject.

She was shaking inside, her mouth dry, her pulse racing. To take meant risk—risking her heart, maybe even her life. To reject meant locking herself away from a life worth living.

She took. It was sheer instinct; the inner voice had no time to intervene. Only to react once it was too late. *I hope you know what you're doing.*

But she had no idea what she was doing, just this crazy instinct to trust him. She rinsed the berries and covertly watched Cody make a loop through her living room. He was taking it all in, from the second-hand couch to the desert scenes she'd cut out of an old calendar to decorate the walls. Everything was improvised, like the scrap of cardboard evening out the legs of the rickety table. God, what would he think?

He leaned over a framed photo. "Nice dog."

*A trick! A trick! Be careful!*

"Buddy," she said, smiling automatically.

"Buddy?" he laughed.

"Hey, I was nine when I named him!" Her hands went to her hips, prompting Cody to throw his palms up in surrender. "He was the best."

He studied the picture more closely then shot her a skeptical look. "Him?"

That dog had been closer to her than most of her family members. A shoulder for her to cry on through her parents' divorce and subsequent remarriages to partners who gradually pushed Heather away. From her ninth birthday until that awful day a decade later when Buddy died, he'd always been there for her.

"The absolute best."

Cody's eyes danced. "Better than Lassie?"

She laughed. He'd chosen the right moment to lighten things up. She was much too tense. "Way better."

"Better than Rin-Tin-Tin?"

"A totally different class."

He raised his eyebrows. "What about Benji? Benji could solve crimes, you know." His eyes sparkled at some inside joke.

She shook her head, unimpressed. "Buddy didn't need to solve crimes; he was so good at keeping trouble away."

"Big dog." Cody shook his head skeptically.

"I like big dogs."

His head tilted to one side. "How big?"

"Big." What was this, some kind of Freudian analysis? She moved from the kitchenette, holding out the bowl of strawberries, willing her hand not to shake. "Dessert?"

Cody grinned, and she immediately felt her face heat in a flush.

*Never trust any man!* the fearful voice cried. But this time, the voice came from a distance, as if it had been grabbed by the scruff of its neck and was being escorted out the back door, fading away into the night. *Don't trust anyone...*

Cody snagged a strawberry and continued his inspection, tilting the photo of Heather and Cathy to the light. The two of them in uniform, hockey sticks crossed. "Field hockey, huh?"

She forced a light tone even as her gut clenched at the memory of Cathy. "I played in college."

"Let me guess. Defense."

Heather frowned. Did she really come across that way? Wary, on guard? She shook her head. "Midfield." The ones who covered the most miles. Like she'd done her whole life.

"You look dangerous with that stick."

"You better believe it." She faked a chuckle. "It's still in my car, actually. I never get around to taking it out." She left out the rest—how it filled some of the emptiness of the backseat with Buddy gone. Buddy, with his long ears, flopping in the breeze.

"I'll make sure to be good." He looked at Heather like she was the next photograph to study, and then snagged another berry.

Pulse spiking, she ducked around him and slid the patio door open with a screech. Normally, she kept herself locked up at night, but some irrepressible urge called to her. Mesquite from the neighbor's barbecue wafted in along with the nutmeg-vanilla flavor of the night-scented flower. It was the scent of a vast space. The scent of possibility.

"Scorpio's up," Cody said, a whisper at her shoulder. His scent joined the others. Distinctly Cody, it was like the beach at midnight: warm and inviting. But danger wasn't far off, not with this man. She could feel the coiled power in him. Around him, almost. Like a force field. Maybe if she stood close enough, it would protect her, too.

That, or it would kill her with one electrifying jolt.

She had the distinct feeling he was sniffing her. One in ten hairs on the back of her neck stood; the other nine cheered. She wouldn't mind sniffing him back. Inhaling, actually, right at the crook of his neck.

A hand reached around her and teased the pile of strawberries before selecting one. It moved right past her ear and
turned into a luscious sound even as the scent of it made her
mouth water. She could picture his lips closing around the
strawberry, fingers tugging the stem free. Oh, to dance with
this man again. To lose her fears in those arms. The physical
beckoned, not just as a thrill but as a gateway to more. But
how, how to proceed?

The couple of men Heather had slept with had all started as
friends. A one-thing-led-to-another-and-then-we-were-naked
kind of thing. She'd never slept with a stranger; never let
things get wild after too many drinks or a few heated looks.
Cody was not quite a stranger, but not quite a friend. Yet the
desert kept whispering his name to her, again and again.

She closed her eyes and listened. A faraway voice had joined
the whisper. Voices? No, yips—the sound of coyotes, howling
in the distance. Heather's eyes searched as if the high fence
around her drab yard weren't blocking the view. She imagined
the coyotes, lined up along a scrubby ridgeline, muzzles pointed
high. She loved that sound. It was one reason she didn't need
a TV or stereo out here: the desert was entertaining enough.
The crickets were the newscasters, the lizards starred in action
movies. Birds sung arias, and the coyotes—they played full
symphonies. They were warming up now, voices honing in on
the right key.

"Funny," Heather murmured, "Until I got to Arizona, I
thought coyotes only howled at a full moon."

Cody snorted. "Common misconception. They howl any-
time it feels right. When the night tells them to."

The idea went down her soul like a warm drink. Doing
what felt right. Following the night. If only she could do the
same. Standing this close to Cody felt right, and what the
night was suggesting. . . Well, she hadn't been this tempted in
a long time.

Heather waited for the warning voice to butt in and ruin
everything, but there was only silence from that quarter. She
spied on Cody from the periphery of her vision, watching him
listen to the coyotes with closed eyes. His face twitched in

response to each variation in the song, as if he were following a conversation. A smile, a nod, a tilt of the head. What was it about this guy?

He was the picture of a man in his element, a man at home. What she wouldn't give to have that feeling. She'd spent her childhood shuttling between homes and summer camps. The only place she ever felt she belonged was the hockey field. A delineated green rectangle. Lucky man, Cody. The place where he belonged was magical, almost mystical.

Part of his aura suggested the place belonged to him. She'd felt that on the ranch, time and again. The man had that natural authority, that statement of right. But he was restless, too. What would it take to make him complete?

She turned and set the strawberries aside, facing Cody, an inch away. Wishing desperately for him to start what they both wanted. He held back, though, letting her take the lead, even if the hitch in his breath gave the effort of it away. She loved him for it, but hated what it said about her. Did she really come off as so fragile?

God, maybe she was. Being attacked in an alley on a dark Friday night will do that to a girl. For once, the memory made her bristle with fresh determination instead of cower. She had escaped that alley. Started a new life. Here. Now.

Heather stepped forward and put a hand on Cody's chest. Beneath the soft cotton of his shirt was solid steel that heated at her touch. Half-closing her eyes, she tilted her head and wished for his lips. Imagined them brushing over hers, soft and sweet. She saw his eyes drop to her lips and focus there as if he were counting her breaths, waiting for his chance. The way the girls did at school, studying the beat of a jump rope before leaping in. Waiting... waiting...

The coyotes warbled on, high and hopeful, then low and lonely.

She'd had enough of waiting and wishing. Enough of lonely. On the next breath, Heather reached for his lips with her own.

# Chapter Eight

Heather put everything into that kiss—all her joy, her sorrow, her hope. She squeezed her whole body to his, savoring the sweet taste of strawberry on his lips. Arms banded with muscle circled her waist, and she wove her arms behind his neck. The man was a fireplace on a cold winter's night, emanating warmth and security.

A pause, a breath. He was waiting for her. God, she needed help with this. How to proceed?

"Cody, help me," she whispered, threading her fingers into his hair.

His face took on that Huck Finn grin. "With what?"

"You know what."

His lips moved to her ear. "Pretend I don't."

She inhaled and tried to summon the old Heather from deep inside. "Cody, I want you." Just that whisper stirred the need burning inside her.

His lips teased her ear. "You want me to..?"

She shifted her jaw, gathering her nerve. He needed a clearer message? Fine! She'd give it to him. She plunged into a deep, wet kiss and gave herself an inner nod. How's *that* for assertive? When she pulled back, Huck Finn was gone, and a very surprised Cody stood in his place.

She admired her courage for all of three seconds before throwing herself in for another taste of him. She was addicted already, after only that touch. As for Cody, his lips went from surprised to hungry, and his arms pulled her tight. Every inch of her body found a home on him, snug and warm. Something inside her was welling up. Something—or everything, all at once: joy, sorrow, want, need, all of it finding expression in a soft moan.

Cody kissed her right through it then pulled back with a sharp intake of air—a diver bursting to the surface after venturing too deep. He rested his forehead against hers for a long, quiet moment, seeming to pull himself together. "You're getting me ahead of myself," he whispered, gulping back the ragged edge in his voice. "How about we do this right?" he murmured, lips moist on her ear.

*Right* was just what Heather needed. Right now. She nodded, eyebrows rubbing against his chin, watching his smile stretch. He was looking down at her, eyes dancing on hers. Another kiss, more measured this time, and then his mouth teased her ear. "We need to finish that dance, you know."

She slid back into him again, held him close, and felt his foot shift, his body sway. Something vibrated against her chest: a hum, slow and steady, coming from him. They slow danced in place for a moment until he raised one hand and let the other gently guide her through a turn. Then he tucked her close again, her back against his chest, thick arms crossed over her.

Heather stood, practically purring as he repositioned his hands by her hips. "Touch me," she heard herself whisper, pushing his hands under her shirt and up from the neutral zone of her waist to her lower ribs. *Nice*, she thought then mumbled it aloud. He let out a chuckle and stroked until she nudged him higher.

"Here?" His voice rumbled through her torso, hands easing higher.

"Everywhere." That drew another smile. She could feel it on her ear.

She held her breath as Cody's fingers worked over the swell of her ribs to the edge of her bra. He traced it as his mouth massaged the soft juncture of her shoulder and neck. One of his hands lifted and went to her hair, combing it so gently, she could have sighed. His mouth played at the skin of her neck, soft, then hard, until he broke off with an audible intake of air. She wanted more, but he just smoothed the hair over her neck and anchored his nose by her ear. His hands became her focus again, as they inched slowly from her ribs to the curves of her breasts.

"Here?" Cody whispered.

"Mmmm," was all she could manage. Her core was already weeping in anticipation. This man wasn't just a long-lost friend, he was a long-lost lover, and she'd been missing him for more than a lifetime. Cody circled her nipples through the fabric of her bra and she bit her lip, holding back a moan of delight. Her breasts were swelling, filling his hands, marveling at how different this was. Heather joined in, echoing his movements with her own thumbs. Until now, her sexual encounters had been giggly, fun. This was all heat, irresistible desire that had her leaning forward, pulling her shirt over her head, and tossing it aside.

Her body was in full meltdown mode, leaning back into him, giving herself away. Because she wanted—no, she needed this. Deserved it, even. A little tenderness in a life that had somehow become all about survival.

Just when she couldn't stand one more minute of slow and sweet, he tugged her hands above her head and turned her in a pirouette that finished with them face-to-face, mouth-to-mouth. As their tongues began their own slow dance, her fingers tangoed down the buttons on his shirt. Now her hands were sliding over skin, bumping over muscle. Pushing the shirt back over his shoulders, she couldn't help rounding them a second and third time, drinking her fill of his barely restrained power. He could have grabbed her and pinned her down. He could have taken over the kiss, the dance. But he didn't. He let her dictate the pace—and she soared with the confidence he gave her.

He clasped her hands in his next, guiding them up and around, turning her back to him. The curves of her body meshed perfectly with his. What was it he said when they first danced? *We're made for each other.* Must be true, because she'd always had two left feet—until now. He slipped his fingers inside her bra then discarded it completely. A half turn later, she had his shirt off. Bodies ever closer, ever hotter. Another turn, another layer. She was a ballerina atop a music box, part instinct, part art. Her shorts slid to the floor, one inch at a time, followed by his jeans in a slow-motion feast.

Two more half turns stripped away panties, then boxers. God, this was nothing—nothing!—like one-thing-led-to-another. This was deliberate, inevitable. As if fate had scripted it all along, holding back her heart so it could cave in completely tonight, all over this man. Her lips tiptoed along his neck then suckled the same point he'd been so fixated on before on her own neck. She could feel his pulse quicken, right under the skin. Under her hands, his ass was firm, corded. She was about to curl a leg around his hips and press herself to his erection when Cody went back to slow and easy, shifting into the maddeningly unhurried pace of an overprotective bear. Didn't he know she wouldn't break or wither or cry? All she wanted was him—all of him. Now.

"Cody, please," she moaned.

His breath tickled her neck. A kiss, a whisper. "Soon."

His hands gripped her hips and squeezed her close. She could feel his cock pushing, her body responding. His hands traveled leisurely over her breasts then meandered down to her hips, curving closer to her sex. Conflicted in their greed, her hips pushed forward toward his hands then back against his cock.

Heather thought she had sworn off men. Ha! This one, she wanted to swallow whole. "Cody." It was meant to be a whisper but came out in a moan.

His hands explored the curls of her pelvis, sinking deeper then dancing away.

"Cody, please." God, she was begging him. But did she care?

No. Not when he was mouthing her name into her ear, again and again. Not when he was worshiping her body with every unsteady breath he drew. The man was a Midas of the soul, turning everything in her to gold. Mining now, finding her pussy. One finger slid inside, then another. Heather worked an arm behind her and closed on a column of hot desire, living marble that pulsed under her touch. A single spot of moisture pressed into her tailbone. His fingers curled inside her, circling and widening her, then probing deeper. Heather teetered on the verge of a very deep canyon. Falling now, crying out as everything inside her convulsed in need. Was it possible to come so quickly? With Cody, anything seemed possible. But drawing this out would be so much better than rushing through, so she fought to regain control even as her body begged to let it all go.

Cody held her, snug and patient. Slowing long enough for her to pull her wayward nerves back together. The blur of the patio doors came into focus again, and suddenly, she wanted it all. No longer a ballerina but a woman possessed, she turned in his arms. Her kiss went deep, demanding, her leg winding around his.

Cody growled. An actual growl. "Bedroom?"

She shook her head. "Right here. Now."

He chuckled at that then slid his arms around her, taking her weight and lowering both of them to the rug. Was the man an ice skater in his spare time, used to maneuvering women through the air? Her legs parted, her heels climbed his calves, then his thighs. Of their own volition, her arms stretched overhead as if waiting to be twirled once again. He took her hands in his and held on tight.

Heather couldn't rate what happened next, it was so far off her charts. The feel of his cock, teasing at her entrance while his eyes found her pleading *yes.* The warm slide of him, inside at last. His exhale on her cheek, the sound of a swallowed moan. Hers was much less subtle. And why should it be? Her soul was skipping with more than the physical rush of his cock sliding along her inner walls. Slow, hot, heavy.

"Condom," he murmured, rising.

"Stay!" A desperate plea. She pushed her hips up and saw his eyes flutter. She let her sheath grip hard and milk him until he pushed deep again, his entire body quivering. Hers, too—so much, she had to suck back a lusty hiss.

His weight shifted again. "Be right back."

She clutched at the space he vacated, aching at the sudden loss. But he was back in an instant, smoothing the condom over his length. She wanted to unroll it herself but was too shaky to manage. Next time.

Cody grinned at her exactly then, maybe reading her mind. So she thought it again, and harder. She wanted lots of next times. The patio curtain wafted in the breeze and tickled her leg, seconding that plan. His jaw scrubbed along her cheek; she'd take that as a yes, too.

When he slid back in, it was the first rain after a long drought. The sensation flooded her as Cody rocked ever harder, sweat gleaming on his chest. Heather found herself pumping in time with him, hips lifting right off the floor. That she was somehow doing it right was evident in the glow building in his eyes. A real glow, like an animal in the night. Heather put that down to her sensual state. She was seeing stars and all manner of pulsing lights, so why not a glow? It filled her eyes even when she closed them, feeling him plunge deeper, so hard and fast it should have hurt. But Heather was soaring, wrapped so tightly around him that when his climax shook him, it took her, too. Carrying her away, deep into the night.

# Chapter Nine

Round one was a dream; round two took them to the bed. On one breath, Heather inhaled Cody's sea breeze scent. On the next, she drifted into sleep.

Into the nightmare.

"Tonight we're living dangerously," Cathy declared.

Every time she replayed the nightmare, it started with those words. If only she had screamed her warning then.

Why she had listened to Cathy, she didn't know. Wild Friday nights in techno bars were really not her thing. Or maybe that's why she did it, because how often could she turn down her best friend's admonitions to get out on the town?

"I can't wait for you to meet Alon," Cathy squeaked, primping her hair. She'd been talking about him all week, using terms like aristocratic, steamy, and hot. "And he's got friends!" She winked.

The dim bar was jamming, a crush of bodies swaying in the dark. The beat of the music so loud, Heather could almost felt it pushing the blood through her veins. She was barely through the door before she started looking for a way out.

"There he is!" Cathy motioned to the back of the bar and plowed through the crowd, a woman possessed. Two men stood there, shadows against the far wall. They were tall and angular, with raven-black hair that shone, even in the shadows. Delicately chiseled cheekbones on strangely pale cheeks gave them the look of elite male models. But Heather didn't find them hot in the least. An icy feeling gripped her throat as they eyed her approach. She wanted to turn and run right there. Wanted to grab Cathy and go.

Too late. "Alon!" Cathy practically leaped into a kiss. He let her, but his eyes were on Heather. And didn't let go all night.

Not when she went to the bathroom, telling herself to calm down. Not when she deliberately maneuvered away from him at the table. Every inch she gained, he sucked back up. The man was a black hole, spinning her way, and she was flailing helplessly in a vacuum.

"Heather," Alon said, lacing every letter with greed. The man barely breathed, barely moved. He was a coiled cat, studying its prey with hypnotizing eyes. "Tell me about yourself, Heather." Something inched into her as he spoke. A potion, a poison, she didn't know what. Only that it was hard to focus on anything but his face. Her mind was distant, almost dull. The only thing that really registered was a warm shot of lust when Alon leaned into her space, eyeing her neck. His nostrils flared, and he exchanged a look with his friend.

If it hadn't been for the fire door beside them opening, Heather would have closed her eyes and let him close in. But the cool, fresh air slapped her back into thinking. Jesus, had the man spiked her drink?

*Out! Get the hell out!* She tried pulling Cathy with her, but the woman's eyes were vague, lusty. Bewitched. Another tug, but Cathy just slapped her hand away. Alon's face curled in a cold smile, and Heather backed away, plunging through the crowd and out the fire door. After the stuffy bar, the crisp air of the street was a relief. She felt cleaner, clearer as she gulped the fresh air.

Until the bar door swung open. "Leaving so soon?" Alon's voice was deep, silky.

She spun and speed-walked away, barely holding back from a run. A glance back revealed only shadows. When she faced forward again, he was there. Right in front of her, one hand pinching her arm. Shock rooted her in her step. How did the man move so fast?

He reached out and stroked her cheek, and the touch was cold and clammy. Reptilian. His nails were perfectly groomed, his skin, an unnaturally smooth alabaster. Like a deer in headlights, bracing for impact, Heather waited for her doom. His hand brushed her hair behind her ear, smoothed her neck. Why couldn't she move? Why couldn't she scream? The hand was behind her now, pulling her close as his head tilted. A glint of red rimmed his eye and his teeth—his fangs—flashed white.

Heather stopped breathing. Almost stopped thinking. Then survival instinct struck her and she struggled to break free. He only smiled and gripped her harder, fingernails digging deep.

That's what did it, that pinch. It snapped her together just long enough to ram a knee into his groin and twist her wrist free. She stumbled away, horrified at the hungry flicker in his eyes. The look of a hunter, eager to play.

If it hadn't been for the half-drunk bachelor party that staggered around the corner then, Heather would be dead.

"Hey baby, join the party!" One of them grabbed her arm and pulled her along. She went willingly, feeling Alon's eyes bore into her back, right down the alley and around the next corner. Even there, she could feel his presence reaching for her.

A police car rolled by, and she nearly screamed for help. But what would they say to a woman straight out of a bar, reporting a vampire? They'd probably book her, not him. So she ran all the way home, bolted the door, and yanked down every shade. She'd ended up locked in the bathroom all night, phone in one hand, kitchen knife in the other, wishing desperately that Buddy had lived longer, if only to see her through this awful night.

A tickling sensation where Alon had grabbed her neck told her she was anything but free. More like a fox released just long enough to make for a better chase. His eyes had promised as much.

Throughout that night, Heather called Cathy every half hour without a response. She called her all the next day, and every minute, another of her nerves frayed through. Finally, she steeled herself and went to Cathy's apartment. The police were there amidst teary neighbors who shook their heads and tsked. *A terrible crime.* The woman had her wild ways, they whispered, but she didn't deserve this. To be raped, beaten, ritualistically bled.

Cathy was dead, a victim of some sadistic group. What kind of monster would do something like that? No one could say.

No one but Heather.

Within an hour, she'd thrown a couple of hastily packed bags into her car, withdrawn as much cash as her cards would allow, and hit the highway. Heading somewhere, anywhere. Away from the red-rimmed eyes that pierced the night. The ones staring at her now, as she slept.

She jackknifed up, screaming. Her heart was racing by the time she realized that the red came from her alarm clock, and the hands were Cody's, callused and calm. But the wingbeats outside were real—the sound of bats taking flight. Had they been hanging around her roof again? Heather collapsed into Cody's chest. He curled around her, whispering softly. If that solid body couldn't shield her from harm, nothing could.

He'd check her into the nearest mental ward if she said it. Vampires. No, she wouldn't say a word. She'd run from that world and into his, and damn it, she'd take refuge as long as she could.

# Chapter Ten

Cody breathed in Heather's sweet scent and held her close. Tight as his arm was around her chest, she squeezed it even closer a dozen times in the night until she'd fallen asleep, peace inching its way cautiously through the consuming darkness.

It took him another hour to get to sleep after that. His canines pushed at his gums and every muscle roared for the blood of whoever created that nightmare. He'd find the scum, rip him limb from limb. But he had to force his wolf down— again. The beast had nearly fought his way out twice tonight. First in the temptation to mark her as his mate, and now with the urge to destroy an unknown enemy. But there was a right way of doing things and a wrong.

He wouldn't give Heather the mating bite until she wanted it as desperately as he did and understood what it meant. Neither could he kill the enemy until he knew where to direct his rage. Right now, all he could do was soothe and protect. Love her, as he'd never loved anyone before. Even if it killed him to wait.

He took solace from that scent—his and hers, intertwined. He'd have to scrub her good and hard in the shower before he let her go to work. Much as he wanted to shout it to the world, no one could know about them. Not yet.

Her heart beat steadily under his hand. When she stirred, he kept his eyes shut, wondering what she would do. He'd gone to bed with plenty of women. But waking up with one? He'd never tried that. Never even been tempted. But with Heather, it seemed totally natural. Instinctual even.

Not a good thing, because every thought, every responsibility had fled his mind the minute he walked through her door.

How was he ever going to earn his father's respect if he was distracted by a woman? He couldn't afford that now.

His wolf gave a grumpy snarl. *She helps us. We keep her!*

Cody fought back a response. *Damn it, I want to keep her, too! I just have to keep my head screwed on!*

An internal snarling match ensued that only died down when Heather's muscles shifted then flexed. When she slid away, hair brushing his shoulder, his wolf nearly let out a whine. Cody calmed the beast, determined to see what she would do. Would she bury her face in her hands and shed tears of regret? Hide in the bathroom for an hour then breeze out to work, pretending nothing had happened? Would she—

A kiss. A long, silky kiss, right on his cheek, one that sang with barely restrained hope. Just that light touch was enough to set his heart hammering. It was all he could do not to reach out for more or promise her everything.

Cody gulped. If this woman wasn't destined for him, no one was.

The pad of her finger made a slow, lingering journey over his shoulder, leaving a warm trail that reached his bones. It traced the curves of his ear, lingering over the scar, then smoothed his eyebrow. If there was anything better than making love to her, this might be it. He could have howled when it ended, the bed shifting as she stood. Cody fought hard to control the growing desperation of his inner wolf, who wanted to tug her back and keep her close. *Mine!*

He managed to keep all that down and only crack open one eyelid. In the fire of dawn, Heather was practically glowing. She took two steps across the tiny cottage, fumbled with the coffee maker, then reached for some clothes. So soon? Was she ready to let this night pass?

Maybe not entirely because she hesitated, and then dropped the clothes. Gloriously naked, she stepped out the back door. It was a sight reserved for Cody's eyes only, thanks to the high stockade fence surrounding the small property. She unrolled a mat and settled cross-legged on it, arms reaching up to frame Venus in the pinkish-yellow light of dawn.

Yoga. She was doing yoga. Much as Cody preferred her at his side, he kept still and soaked in the view. With the leisurely stretch of a sleepy cat, she rose and faced the east. A satisfied cat with a full stomach and a warm place to bask. The fear was down to a mere whiff now, the nightmare pushed far, far away. A rush of pride registered in his gut, knowing that part of her calm came from having him there. He could feel it the same way he could feel a solid lump in his chest—one that pulsed with every beat of his heart, whispering. *Home. This is home.* Not the place, but the person. He was sure of it.

Surer still when she let him pad over and sit wordlessly in the doorway with a mug of coffee, watching her. She carried on, a smile playing on her lips as she worked through a series of balances and stretches in a pantomime of nature. She was a waking cat, a steady oak, a hovering bird, each move melting into the next. Dancer, dreamer, beauty: Heather was all of those things.

She came to her knees, reached high, and extended one leg to the side. Reaching her arms wide, she paused, then slowly leaned over the outstretched leg. Palm skyward, she swooped up, hand scooping the air like a flower waking in the desert. Cody found himself suspended between arousal and artistic delight. After she repeated the move on the other side, she straightened on her knees and paused. An invitation?

He lowered his mug to the floor and came over silently to kneel behind her on the mat. He eased into contact, keeping his hands light on her waist. Her skin captured the essence of sunrise: pastel-soft and warm. Her body supple, contoured just right for his frame. His heart skipped when she resumed the routine, making him part of her. As she leaned left and held the stretch, he ran a finger down the inside of her outstretched arm, holding his breath the whole time. Like a bird stretching its wings, she swept upward. He was beneath those wings now, marveling at their grace. His hands went back to her ribs, light, loose, not wanting to interfere with her flight. Stretch, slide, up; he echoed each of her moves then added his own.

A kiss on the shoulder, a brush of her breast. Heather continued her routine, quivering now. He cupped her breasts, feeling them lean and lift as she went through the moves. He could smell her desire, taste her pleasure. It was dizzying, knowing what he could make her feel, knowing the power she wielded over him at the same time. He licked a finger and worked her nipples until they were hard and high, visibly straining for more. His chest was against her back now, ears tuned to her breath. They were slow, steady breaths that he would have copied if he weren't afraid to let out a groan. So he worked his lips against a smooth shoulder instead. There. He'd forsake oxygen for the next few minutes and breathe in Heather instead.

She settled into a seated position, the soles of her feet meeting as her knees dropped apart. For all her tension last night, she was now sage and serene. He settled behind her, cradling her between his legs. A thrill went through him when she leaned back and pushed her knees wider, inviting him to explore. His fingers slid slowly, gradually, past her curls and into her folds. That might have been pushing the boundaries of yoga, but damned if he could hold back. Not when he reached her wet, welcoming pussy. Not when she leaned back, begging him for more. As he teased her inner thighs, Heather's steady breaths wavered. Cody closed his eyes. He didn't need to see to find the bud of her clit, didn't need to hear to pick up her inner cry of delight at the contact.

Jesus, what made this so different from every other time he'd pleasured a woman? Was it that fact that the pleasure was shared, an even split? That every sharp breath she took was matched by a tremble of his own? That had to be it. This was making love, not a quick, hard fuck.

His inner wolf growled as if the word *fuck* had suddenly offended his sensibility.

And the wolf was right. The minute emotion got added to the equation—because hell, it was impossible to keep his heart locked away—*fuck* no longer applied. Not to his mate.

She was perfect. They were perfect. The morning was perfect—but damn, it was already slipping away. How to maintain this languid pace, even as the sun rose, and his cock with it? How to preserve the serenity of the moment? His fingers circled her cunt, coaxing it wide. He wanted to drive into her right away, lose himself in her sweet tunnel. But for her, he'd force himself to go slow, to explore deeper. He'd coax another dozen sighs and moans out of her before letting himself go, even if his cock was about to explode.

Together, they danced along the edge of all-out desire, inventing a whole new series of moves. All of it unspoken, uncued, the two of them perfectly in tune. She leaned back, far back, dripping slowly from his lap onto a puddle on the mat. He rolled onto her without breaking contact, and paused, cock straining at her entrance, savoring the glory of the moment.

He mimicked the easy pace of her yoga moves, sliding into her gradually and relishing every inch of her slick heat. A pleasure so new, so intense, it hurt. He retreated, slower than slow, then dipped back in. In, in, in. God, he was so in. Heart and soul on the line, and there was nothing he could do but hang on for the ride. Somehow, though, he stopped long enough to stop, duck inside, and grab a condom in record time. Then he slid back into position and picked up where he left off.

Slow and delicious quickly became deep and delicious, then deep and hard as Heather urged him to fill her, again and again. Her legs wrapped tightly around him, her breath ragged. He gloried in watching her come, once, twice, until the sun was slanting over the fence, hurrying them along. Only then did he give in to the urge, hammering home with the power he'd been holding back all morning. She was utterly open to him, arms overhead, neck exposed. Her pulse throbbed at the juncture of shoulder and neck. There—right there! He could claim his mate and solve everything with one bite! He could—

No. If he claimed her now, she'd be little more than a slave to him for the rest of her life. He would have to hold on for the day when she gave herself willingly to his bite. Cody locked his teeth behind his lips and channeled the urge to his hips instead, penetrating again and again. Heather matched his rhythm, locking down hard on his cock, half-lost in sensual delirium. Higher and higher they flew, until he slammed over a peak and spilled his passion into her with a cry. Panting, hearts thumping, they eventually dropped back, nuzzling.

"Good morning," Heather breathed into his ear, looking more serene than he'd ever seen her. He wanted to give her lots of good mornings, one after another all the way to the end of his life.

A pang hit him amidst the joy of the moment. This was Monday, not Sunday morning, and they were out of time. But that was the least of it. Heather wasn't a wolf. She was human. And he was the alpha's son, a man expected—no, required— to find a suitable mate. A shifter female of high standing. Nothing else would do.

He wound his arms around Heather and tucked her head under his chin. Destined mates? Or destined for heartbreak? Cody shielded his face from the encroaching sunlight. Soon, the day—and reality—would be upon them.

For better or worse.

# Chapter Eleven

A hint of strawberry teased at Cody's lips as he drove home. He tucked them in, savoring the reminder of his first night with Heather. If she hadn't had to go to school, he could have stayed there all day. But there was work to be done, a case to crack.

He detoured to check in with Kyle, who carefully refrained from any comment as to where his houseguest might have spent the night, and then drove to the ranch on the pretense of reporting to Ty. What Cody really wanted was to be near Heather. And what he needed to ask Ty had nothing to do with the case.

Cody parked and pretended to sniff the healthy ranch air on the short walk to Ty's place. He honed in on Heather's scent, coming from the schoolhouse. The edgy feeling he'd had since parting with her dissipated. She was close. She was safe.

*Mine!* his wolf added.

*Ours,* the man agreed with an inner nod.

He turned the corner of his brother's house and skidded to a halt. Ty was there, all right, leaning back in a patio chair, his face lathered with shaving cream. Lana was bent over him, sliding a straight-edged razor along his jaw, their legs practically intertwined. Judging by the heated sparks between them, this close shave would end very close, indeed.

"Uh, Ty?" Cody ventured as something behind his ribs twinged at the sight. He'd never once in his life been jealous of Ty—not the power, not the responsibility. But this—this sweet serenity, this stamp of forever—it almost hurt to see. If Cody didn't know better, he'd have sworn his brother was purring. Until, of course, Ty growled.

"One of these days—" Ty started.

"Don't move." Lana whipped the razor away and clamped a hand around her mate's chin. "Hi, Cody."

He could see his brother's Adam's apple bob then settle. Behind the lather on his tanned face, the color rose. *One of these days, Cody, I am truly going to kill you.*

Cody gave an exaggerated sigh. *Give me a time when the two of you aren't going at each other.*

*Give me a time when we get any privacy,* Ty shot back.

For a minute, the only sound was the slow scrape of the razor on Ty's skin, the distant buzz of a bee.

"Where's my favorite niece?" Cody tried.

Lana smiled. "Feeding horses with my grandmother." She tipped Ty's head to the side and started on his neck, a definite gleam in her eye.

*What do you want, Cody?* Ty growled.

*Heather.* The first thing that popped into his mind. Good thing he didn't let it slip far enough out for his brother to catch.

"Advice," he said.

His brother's eyes slid over to him, studying. Lana took another long scrape before pulling back to look at Ty, then Cody. She wiped the razor clean and slipped wordlessly into the house.

Ty wiped the shaving cream off his lip. "You have two minutes."

Cody pulled a chair over and straddled it backward. He took a deep breath. "How did you know that Lana was...that you and she were...you know..." Ty arched an eyebrow. "Mates."

When Ty leaned in and sniffed, the furrow between his eyebrows deepened. Cody had put considerable effort into masking Heather's scent, but his brother's nose was too good. "You know she's off-limits," Ty said through clenched teeth. "You know you can't."

"So was Lana," Cody blurted. "Didn't stop you." He immediately pulled back, expecting an outburst, like the time he'd made a joke about Ty's phantom—the hint of a mate that haunted his brother for years before he finally found Lana. That joke had earned him the fiercest beating of his life, including a torn ear. He still carried that scar. Had he deserved it? Absolutely. Because now, for the first time, Cody understood what had Ty wound so tight.

But instead of growling, his brother's near-snarl became a smile. An actual smile. "No, I guess it didn't." Then he shook his head and glowered again. "Heather is human, Cody."

"Doesn't matter," Cody insisted.

"I'd say it does. Dad sure as hell will say it does."

"Other wolves have mated with humans."

"Other wolves, yes. But never one of us. Never."

"So?"

"So?" Ty shot it back at him.

A cardinal swooped by, a splash of red in the desert landscape. Cody hung his head. If Heather were a wolf, it would be so easy. She'd know their ways, submit to his bite. They could build a life together, one day at a time.

"Stay away from her," Ty said, his baritone grinding over bedrock. "Focus on the case."

Cody threw up his hands. "I can't stay away. I can't not see her. It's like. . . like the wind purposely carries her scent to me." His shoulders slumped. He could imagine the lecture Ty was about to deliver. *Duty. Maturity. Responsibility.*

Ty took a long time answering, though, studying Cody closely. "You actually mean it." Wonder tinged his words.

"Of course I mean it!" All the frustration of the past years found release in those words. Damn it, what would it take for his brother to take him seriously? "I love her."

Ty chewed on an answer then spit it out. "Might not be enough."

That arrow penetrated Cody's deepest fears. He let out a breath and took a long time finding another. How could he ever explain things to Heather? Could she live with the truth? Suddenly, his father didn't seem like his biggest obstacle any more.

"Watch it," Ty warned. "You break that chair, my mate will kill you."

Cody looked at his hands, clenched white on the back of the frame. He let go with some effort. Wasn't there something around here he could break, throw, or smash?

He could feel Ty's eyes boring into him, looking for the truth. Then from the depths of that glower, a whisper emerged. "If you're serious, I'll back you up."

Good thing he was sitting. His brother was actually offering support? Cody managed a nod, not sure whether his burden had just been eased or increased. "So what do I do?"

Ty shrugged, looking for Lana. Cody's two minutes were up. "Do what you have to do."

That was about as much as he'd get out of his brother. More than he expected, in any case. Cody stood and replaced the chair as Lana reappeared, shaving brush in hand.

"But Cody?" Ty's voice halted his steps.

"Yeah?"

"If you're not serious. . . you're on your own," Ty finished with a murderous look.

Now that was the brother he knew. As Cody scurried away, he saw Lana straddle Ty and get back to work. He gave them three minutes, tops, before they hit the sheets. If they even made it that far.

He gave himself three minutes to pull his act together and figure out what the hell to do next.

# Chapter Twelve

"Miss Luth! Do you know where ghosts swim?"

Heather turned from the geography lesson on the black-board to eleven grinning faces, all anticipating Timmy's punch-line.

"Lake Erie!" he said, sending them all into laughter.

Heather did her best to look stern, cutting him off before he could get on a roll. "Timmy, what did we say about appropriate times to make jokes?"

Timmy tried to look repentant, but it only gave him an endearing pixie effect.

"Right, everyone to learning stations," Heather said, keeping her momentum. "You know where to go?"

A chorus of voices chirped *Yes* as Heather turned on a quiet Mozart fugue. She glanced at the clock; not long before lunch. "Remember, you can talk to your partner, but keep your voices low. Nothing louder than the music. Right, Timmy?" She gave him an extra sharp look.

"Right, Miss Luth!" he shouted, bouncing to the "Europe" station by the windows.

For all that Timmy tested her patience, he was a great kid. Funny, energetic, and sharp. Too bad he kept the latter hidden away while he played his favorite role: class clown. A pity she only had a few more weeks here; give her a school year and she'd bet she could help Timmy work up the confidence to just be himself.

Just like Cody. The man was ingrained in a role, yet so desperate to break free.

Most people grabbed the chance to reinvent themselves the minute they left home, just as she once had. The thing was,

Cody had never really had that chance, not from what she could gather. Family was everything on the ranch, and the kids didn't fly far from the nest. She wouldn't have, either, if she'd grown up in such a utopian place.

So Cody remained stuck in that role—except maybe when he was off the ranch and at her door. She pictured him there, on the threshold to a different persona: the real Cody, emerging like an overcautious turtle from its shell. The Cody nobody knew. She had gotten a few glimpses of that man, and she wanted more. Parting from him that morning had been like breaking their first kiss. It hurt, as if she were up a mountain, struggling to breathe in thin air. She'd had to fight back the feeling with a couple of long yoga breaths. She did the same now, extending the inhale and finding that yes, Cody was somewhere near. Somehow, she could just feel it.

The memories washed over her as she checked on the youngest students, working on their map puzzles. It had been the most beautiful morning of her life, bar none. She'd never had a man kiss her that hard or that soft. Never had a man nuzzle her for a full ten minutes, as if he wanted part of her to rub onto himself. She'd never had a man look into her eyes like he was looking into a crystal ball. And she'd never, ever had that feeling of completion before. That was the stuff of fairy tales, not real life—and certainly not her life. Yet the moment had been hers. Being with Cody chased the fears away.

It wasn't just his bulk or his coiled power, but that watchfulness he exuded, awake and asleep. She'd come out of the shower that morning to find him walking a slow circuit of her tiny yard, inspecting every inch of fence. The man had all but peed on the four corners to mark his territory. His possessiveness should have annoyed her, but she found herself cherishing it. For the first time in her life, she felt protected. Desired. Loved.

A soft knock sounded at the open door, and she opened it to find Cody's sister, Tina, bearing something fragrant and colorful.

"Hi," Tina whispered, waving her over and handing her the gift—a beautiful glass bowl filled with potpourri. The aroma of it filled the schoolhouse, overpowering everything else.

"It's a thank you," Tina said, "for taking on the job and doing it well. We're so glad to have you." She placed the bowl on the front desk. "I think it looks nice here, don't you?"

Heather might have wondered a bit at that, but Lana and Ty had walked by then, Lana's long legs easily keeping pace with her partner's. One of Ty's hands pushed little Tana's tricycle; the other was firmly over Lana's shoulders. Tina smiled and waved at them then winked at Heather with her dark chocolate eyes. "He's gotten very possessive."

Yep, just like Cody and the way he inspected her yard that morning. "They do seem pretty... territorial."

Tina chuckled. "Imagine a pack of dogs," she said. "Better yet, wolves. Our guys are a lot like that."

She smiled. The ranch folk were a clan, friendly yet fiercely protective. Just like Cody. As she watched Lana and Ty, a pang went through her. This morning, she'd had her own tiny taste of that kind of happiness. Dare she wish for more? She caught herself then and threw a worried glance at Tina. Wouldn't do to let on.

But Tina was lost in her own thoughts, watching the couple with eyes so full of yearning that Heather closed her own. Maybe hers wasn't the only heart aching on the ranch today. Dark and intense, Tina was nothing like Cody. Her beauty had an edge to it, like the desert air. Heather recalled the scene at the barn, when Tina and Cody danced. Surely, a woman like Tina would have her pick of a dozen men. Yet she'd been dancing with her brother. Why?

Tina let out an audible sigh then snapped back to herself.

"Why do I have the feeling," Heather said, filling the silence, "that Ty didn't play quite as many pranks as Cody when they were kids?"

Tina laughed out loud. "Ty was always the serious one. It's only since Lana that he's loosened up."

She shot a look at the imposing form. If that was his loose, she'd hate to see the man uptight. No, she'd take Cody any day. Any day or any night. Just the thought sent a ripple through her body.

"Columbus Day weekend is coming up soon," Tina said. "Are you going away?"

She forced a smile. "I'm not sure yet." In truth, she'd been dreading the time off. Work was her anchor to sanity. That and Cody. Would he come back to her tonight? His eyes had been full of unspoken promises that morning when they kissed goodbye. That kiss. . .

"You're from back East, right?" Tina continued. "Any family visiting?"

She wondered what she might say. That there was no one to visit and no one interested in coming to see her? "Um, probably not. They're really busy." Too busy with new lives and new families. "I'll need the time to look for a new job, anyway," she added, sagging at what that meant. Before long, she'd be back on the run.

"We'll hate to see you go," Tina murmured, and then checked her watch. "Oh, I have to run. Time to babysit for a friend."

Heather barely waved in time, too preoccupied. *Back on the run.* The words echoed in her mind as she circulated between learning stations, checking for questions. How long would she be on the run for? Would the nightmare ever end?

*No, no, no,* she told herself. There was only the here, only the now.

Then a small voice spoke from the back of her mind: the old Heather. *There's more. There's Cody. He's worth fighting for.*

But the new Heather trembled and hunched her shoulders, as frightened of hope as she was of the creature that hunted her.

*There's more,* the wind echoed. The words seemed to drift in on a breeze and perch on the rafters, peering down on Heather like a panel of judges. *There's Cody.*

Her heart pounded with the words, circulating them through her body. *Cody. More.*

# Chapter Thirteen

"Cody!"

He whirled, a guilty man. After seeing Ty, he'd spent a few hours making the rounds of the core team of guards. Someone was always on watch at the ranch for all manner of dangers, but it was time to push vampires to the high end of the list. So far, the threat was a distant one, but with vampires on the move... The pack could never be too sure.

He'd just finished up and was making his way to the schoolhouse on a contrived errand—he needed Heather, even just a whiff, a stolen glance from afar—when Tina's voice caught him.

"Cody!"

She was standing on the footpath ahead, bouncing a borrowed baby on her arm, cooing to it in a tone much softer than she used for him. A pity Tina did so much for the pack and so little for herself, really. His eyes narrowed on the baby, then his sister, only to find her giving him the same kind of inquiring look. He had the sneaking suspicion she was on to him and Heather. And the even sneakier suspicion she approved. Why?

The answer should have been obvious, though he'd never really given it thought until now. Tina suffered as much as he did from their father's heavy-handed leadership. Maybe even more. And for all her hard edges, Tina was definitely a closet romantic. A little like Ty.

A little like himself, if he had to admit it. Maybe the three of them had more in common than he thought.

Still floating between despair and elation, he looked to Tina for good news, something to tip the balance. But her grim look told him he was about to be knocked off the tightwire entirely. "Dad wants to see you."

*Shit.*

*Shit, shit, shit.*

Tina gave him a sympathetic look between making baby faces and walked on, talking to the baby. "Now I'll show you your Auntie Tina's office. Won't that be fun?"

"Take me with you?" Cody half-joked. Because a meeting with his father was never a fun thing.

"Forget it, Cody."

"What happened to blood helping blood?" he shot after her.

Tina tossed a firm look over her shoulder. "This is one of those times when you're only my half brother."

"Traitor," he grumbled.

"I heard that."

He sighed. Time to face the firing squad. He squared his shoulders and headed to his father's house. That is, after a detour to the old juniper beside the tool shed, where he rubbed against the trunk like a bull—extra cover for Heather's scent.

Then there was no avoiding it. His father's house was in sight, a bare adobe surrounded by a moat-like ring of knotted thorns. Fitting, really. The man had run off every woman who'd ever dared enter his private life. The place reflected it, a bachelor pad gone gray around the edges. No hummingbirds blurred the air here; instead, a wizened old sentinel of a raven perched outside. Cody knocked, gulped a last breath of fresh air, and entered.

"Cody." His father nodded. The prelude to a lecture, for sure. Cody forced himself to meet the stare of death. It was the same pointless test, every time. *How long will you last this time? How long before you falter?* Sweat beaded on his brow; his cheeks smoldered. That stare could kill. Ty had the same ability, though he usually had the tact to reserve it for enemies. Not so their father. The man was old-school alpha, through and through.

Finally, Cody couldn't hold his gaze any more and dropped his eyes to the floor. Even then, he could feel his father's ever-present scowl.

Silence hung in the room like a raised ax. He steeled himself, wondering what today's lecture might be. That he spent too much money? He had an answer to that one. Over the past three years, he'd built up pretty decent savings, for the first time in his life. Too many women? Not these days, no. And never again, not with Heather in his life. Slacking off on the job? He'd been working his tail off on all that the ranch demanded of him, not to mention perpetually sweeping up the debris left in the aftermath of his father's rough-riding ways. Whatever his father was about to say, he had a response.

"I've decided it's time you took a mate."

He nearly took a step back. Of all the things his father might hit him with, he never expected this. "A mate?"

"A mate. You've had long enough. Time to choose."

His mind spun. Choose? Who? There was only Heather. "Why?" was the best he could manage.

"Look what it's done for Ty."

He didn't know whether to nod or shake his head. Yes, being mated was the best thing that ever happened to his brother. It had pulled Ty back from a near breaking point and given him balance. But that was Ty. Cody didn't need to loosen up.

"Being mated might finally teach you about responsibility."

He wanted to say, *You trusting me more would do that, too.*

"Having a mate is a good thing."

He gave an inward snort. Like his father could talk. The man had led on at least a dozen women without ever committing to one. Fathered four children with two women who'd each run off before his intensity killed them. This was the man lecturing about commitment? The one who snorted at the idea of destined mates?

"You have three months."

*Three months?*

"And if you don't settle on a suitable partner..."

*What, like Lana, who you once threatened with death?*

"...then I will find one for you."

Cody cringed, remembering how his father had once tried finding a match for Ty. Thank goodness that hadn't gone according to the old man's plan. He wondered who his father might deem suitable for him. Beth? Sweet, but not really his type. Audrey? God, no. None of the ranch girls interested him, not in that way.

Only one woman did. The first ever. She'd be his last. His only. Heather.

His wolf let out a ferocious growl. *Mine! Mate!*

The one person his father would never, ever accept. Cody turned for the door, choking on the stuffy air.

"And Cody," his father snapped. "That teacher, what's her name?"

"Heather." As soon as he said it, Cody knew he'd answered too quickly.

His father's eyes flashed obsidian black. "Keep away from her."

All he could manage was a curt nod, telling himself it was a nod of goodbye and not a sign of agreement. Then he was out and away, speed-walking past a blurry landscape, stomach a knot of rusty steel. He flung open the door to his truck, climbed in, and backed out in a roar. He sped out the ranch gate, not caring about the dust cloud it kicked up. All he wanted was some form of escape.

Heather.

Human.

Forbidden.

The words played over and over as he drove, half-blind to his surroundings. Going somewhere, anywhere, he replayed every harsh look his father ever shot him, every disappointed sigh.

He did manage to point the car in the direction of Kyle's office and spend a couple of hours there. But all he accomplished was growling at false leads—not to mention Kyle—before heading back out on the road, his mind fixed on Heather. What the hell was he going to do?

His wolf gave an inner huff. *Do what feels right. What the night tells you to do.*

The next time Cody blinked, the sun had set, and he was at Heather's front door.

# Chapter Fourteen

Heather knew that knock. She'd already sensed his approach somewhere deep in her bones. She flung the door open, trying to rein in her delight. Cody, back at her door.

But the Cody standing there tonight was different. Brooding, dark—as dark as she'd ever seen him. Darker, even. She had already guessed he had that side to him, but he kept it hidden behind the mask.

*Danger! Run away!* the voice of fear trembled.

Heather looked closer. It wasn't the sinister kind of dark. There was something serious about to burst out from behind the facade. He hid it immediately, though, pasting on his show smile. Why did he do that? If he couldn't be himself with her, maybe she didn't deserve him.

"Hey, babe," he started in that happy-go-lucky, Huck Finn way. "I was in the neighborhood and figured we could—"

She shook her head. That was not her Cody. "Try again," she murmured. With a gentle touch, she eased him back and closed the door.

Her heart was pounding, her veins ready to burst. Was she insane? The man she was born to love was at her door, and she was pushing him away when all she wanted to do was drag him in and never let go. Another part of her, though, stood firm. Cody needed to find his own way out of his cage.

The closed-door routine was something she did in school. If a student came in doing something wrong—being too rough or rowdy—she'd turn them around, close the door, and let them try again. It was the kind of second chance that real life rarely offered.

Except this was no schoolboy. He was a man, a fine, fine specimen of a man who could knock on any woman's door on any night and get exactly what he wanted. But she didn't want to be just another door that opened on command. She wanted more. Even in her tension, she smiled. Maybe the old Heather was clawing her way back to the surface, after all.

His second knock sent her nerves fluttering. She swung open the door and held her breath.

Cody still wore the color of surprise. His mouth groped for words and finally landed on one. "Hi."

"Hi," she breathed, inwardly cheering him on.

Those perfect lips opened then shut. Opened again. The thousand-watt smile flicked on. "Sorry to bother you, but—"

Nope. She closed the door, though half her muscles wailed.

Silence. Heather prayed she wouldn't hear footfalls, carrying him away. God, another minute and she'd fling open the door, begging for a second chance.

A third knock. Thank goodness for stubborn men. She pulled the door open.

Serious Cody. Intent Cody. A Cody not to be refused. "Heather," he said, lips tight. Now, only now, could she believe that he and Ty were brothers.

"Cody."

He studied her for a long, long time before stepping forward and burying her in an avalanche of a hug. With his face tucked in her hair, the whisper was barely audible. "Heather." For a while, that was it: her name and his fingers flowing through her hair. Then he breathed softly by her ear. "I miss you the minute you're gone."

The words made her chest go tight. Cody held her for an eternity, like a sailor whose ship was about to set sail. She clutched him right back, hard enough to believe that nothing could drag them apart. Behind them, the clock ticked as one minute then another passed. God, she'd missed him, too. Missed him her whole life even if they'd only met now that she was here.

Eventually he pulled back, eyes wandering over her face. He pushed aside a strand of her hair, smoothed it behind her ear. She cupped his face in both hands, trying to understand what troubled him. She wanted to sit him down and urge him to let it out, the way she needed to get everything out. But how could she find the words? Where would she start? *Cody, I wish...* What did she wish? And what was he wishing, with those yearning, mournful eyes?

Cody slid his eyelids down and tugged her close. Seemed like he wasn't ready to reveal his troubles, at least not in words. Last night, after the nightmare, she'd been the same, and Cody had provided the quiet reassurance she needed. Now it was her turn. She squeezed him back, trying to push away the past and future and just live for this moment of peace.

A whisper slipped from her lips. "Every minute without you is a minute too long."

His arms tightened around her, as his lips wrestled with words, losing badly. She shushed him with a finger to the lips and slid a hand along his neck, making him hum and her spirit soar. His body pressed close, promising escape.

Maybe she needed some escape, too. Because a moment later, a pure animal urge engulfed her. Her tongue slipped through his lips, kissing past the actor and down to the man. One hand stayed on his neck, while the other made a determined trip south to stroke his thigh. If she'd had a moment to think, she would have been shocked at herself. But something in the night—in the moon, maybe?—was urging her on.

Licking the sweet, salty taste of him off her lips, she looked him in the eye and found wild desire. A gulp, and then he was crushing her lips with his.

One thing for sure about this crazy night, it would not be sweet and slow.

Good. She was eager, even desperate for him. Grateful when his hands discarded her shirt and bra without ceremony. Right now, she needed him closer than close. His hands were warm as they worked away her shorts, then skied down her backside and scooped her close. Hasty fingers took care of the remaining clothing, and then the two of them were entangled on the floor. Her core flooded in response to his mouth on her nipples as he began to suckle, driving her ever higher.

Just when she thought she would explode with pleasure, Cody's head popped up, pink with shame. "You deserve better," he murmured, lips tickling her skin.

Better than this man? Her finger toyed with the nick in his right ear. "There is no better," she whispered. "Nothing better than being with you." It was the truth. But Cody's eyes slid shut with the weight of responsibility. Had she gone too far? "Cody," she whispered.

He looked up.

"Don't think so much."

It worked, because they collapsed back into kisses until he pulled her up and tumbled to the bed, where they picked up right where they left off. Her legs snaked around his hips, pulling him close. Cody growled—she swore he growled, the hottest sound she'd ever heard—and worked his hands under her, urging her to roll, giving him her back. He smoothed his hands over her skin: an artist considering the canvas of his newest masterpiece.

Starting from her waist, his hands followed the diagonal of her ribs and reached around to tease her aching breasts. Every move was a wish fulfilled. His fingers gently plowed into the cleft of her legs until they found her cunt, already wet and gaping, begging for more. Cody slid his body over hers, lining them up.

Doggie style? His hands were pulling her hips back then bracketing her body on either side. The position had never really done much for her. It had always seemed a bit crude, actually. The couple of times she'd been talked into it in the past, it had been a complete dud.

Must have been the guy. Because the moment Cody cupped her breasts, all doubt fled. His body heat covered her, giving raw and animalistic a whole new appeal. She let out a moan, feeling his cock glide closer.

But good grief—where was her self-consciousness? Where was her pride?

Must have checked it at the state border. Because she truly didn't care.

A single finger stirred her inner walls. "Is this okay?" Cody's lips tickled her shoulder.

"So good," she moaned into the sheets. This wasn't just dipping toes in a pool of molten ecstasy; it was diving into the deep end. Heaven. She found his shaft with one hand and marveled at its size. It was thick and warm, just for her. She was so wet, so ready.

There was a crackle of foil, a pause, and then his thighs brushed her flanks. A flash of heat ripped a cry from her throat when he plunged past her entrance and into her core. Cody hesitated there, quivering for control.

None of that, not now! She wanted wild and crazy and hard.

"Cody! Push! Hard!"

He slammed the rest of the way in and anchored himself there. She clenched tight, wrapping her inner muscles around him. As good as it felt, hearing Cody's pleasured groan was even better. When he withdrew, then thrust back in, she stretched her arms to the wall to brace herself, biting back a cry for more. Her body greeted each thrust gladly, her ankles wrapped around his calves, clamping him close. He was gliding in and out of her now, his hands cupping her breasts. Words spilled into, and then overflowed from Heather's mind. Tenderness. Raw power. Wonder. Only Cody could combine all those things.

She was vaguely aware of him licking her neck near the base where the shoulder curved, as if he were a prospector after a vein of gold. She angled her head away, heeding the instinct to expose her skin, willing him to nip. But Cody bit back a curse at himself and tucked his cheek there instead.

Her focus jumped deep inside where his cock had suddenly dethroned her heart as principal organ of her body. She could feel him all over, whispering in her ear, gripping her hips as she convulsed beneath him. The edge was so close now. She held on as long as she could then cried out and came in a wild spasm that sent him flying, too. Her legs hung on to him through the sensation of tumbling over and over, refusing to let go.

Even when it was over—she knew it must be over—the delight remained. Cody eased his weight over her back, covering her like a thick blanket in the deepest blizzard of winter.

He nestled close and began to nuzzle her neck, rubbing her in long, possessive strokes. She could have grunted in dirty pleasure at each hot slide. When he flopped down beside her, she rolled to face him, hand splayed on that cliff of a chest. His eyes told her she was beautiful; his arms pulled her close. Words were superfluous to the language they were speaking.

Words like trust. Love. Gratitude. They were all there, tucked into the sheets.

But there were other words, too. Anxiety. Frustration. Fear. This magic night was only a temporary reprieve, she knew. Because tomorrow, the real world would be back.

She hid her face in his shoulder. A temporary measure, at best. But it worked—for now.

# Chapter Fifteen

Cody tapped his fingers on the steering wheel all the way down the highway, brow knitted tight. All the joy of his nights with Heather—a whole week of them since that night of the closing door—still didn't solve his problems. If anything, they seemed to have been compounded.

A mate he couldn't have—one who didn't know his true nature.

A series of murders in which every clue came to a dead end.

A brother who cast a long shadow and a father whose gaze never ventured beyond it.

No matter where he searched for a sliver of hope, it all seemed impossible. The more he loved Heather, the more it hurt. She was his destined mate. Some instinctual part of her knew it, too. The way she held on to him and let go of her fear.

*Our mate recognizes us*, his wolf purred in approval.

All well and good, but how do you tell a human you love her? How do you explain who you really are? Cody worked his jaw from side to side. Every minute he let tick by without telling her was a lie.

Meanwhile, he and Kyle had been up and down the state, hunting down every possible lead but coming up empty. Where would the vampires strike next? The next victim was out there, ignorant of her fate, and Cody could do nothing to save her. His mind spun it over a million times, all the way to the ranch.

Before he knew it, his truck passed under the gate. *Hmpf.* Some jerk had taken his usual spot—a truck he didn't recognize with Nevada plates. Grinding his teeth, he parked two spots away, annoyed as hell that his father had summoned him to a meeting now. He needed to get back to town and finish the job. The sooner he could track down the vampires, the sooner he could concentrate on winning over his mate. Time was running out.

He entered the council room with a quick step then pulled up short. His father stood with another man, a grizzled old alpha. Roric, if Cody remembered correctly, head of the Westend pack, three hundred miles northwest. Beside Roric stood a petite brunette whose appraising eyes latched right on to Cody. The hair on the back of his neck stood up.

"Ah, Cody!" His father was suspiciously jovial. Cody felt the blood drain from his face. "You remember Roric."

He gave a curt nod as Roric's slow lookover did its best to rough him up at ten paces.

"And his daughter, Sabrina." His father practically sang the introduction.

"Hello Cody," she cooed, undressing him with her doe eyes.

"Roric and I have some business to discuss," his father continued. "Why don't you take Sabrina for a walk? Show her around."

His gut twisted, guessing exactly what kind of business his father had in mind. From the gleam in Sabrina's eye, she was fully supportive.

*What happened to three months?* he protested. *What happened to—*

His father's voice boomed in his head. *Think I'll let my son ruin his life?* Cody's blood ran cold as his father's tone grew more measured. *Lest you allow yourself to be distracted by an unsuitable female, I've found you a good one. Isn't she beautiful?*

Maybe before Heather—maybe—he might have sniffed briefly in Sabrina's direction. But now? He felt nothing but the dread spreading through the pit of his stomach.

*But I don't want her,* his inner voice cried.

*You will do as I say!* his father thundered. *Take her, now!*

The double meaning cracked through his head as his eyes roamed the room for some escape. Tina was there, her mouth pinched in a tight line. From the looks of it, she'd tried protesting but had been firmly put in her place. Cody looked desperately to Ty. Maybe the two of them together could... But no, Ty's face was a mask. Where was the help he promised?

His mind flailed for some way out, even as he recognized the hard truth. Men like his father and Roric didn't care about love or individual desire. To them, it was all about the pack and bloodlines. Mating was business, pure business, a way to strengthen ties between two allied packs. Had Roric even asked about Rae, who'd been a member of Westend pack before coming to Twin Moon Ranch? He doubted it.

Roric and old Tyrone had tried their callused hands at matchmaking once upon a time, intending Rae as a mate for Ty. The fact that they hadn't consulted either member of the prospective couple never seemed to bother them. Were the old dogs doing it again now?

Cody ground his teeth and glanced at his father. When their eyes met, he nearly reeled from the force of his old man's glare. The fire in those eyes could kill a man, and from the looks of it, his father was more than ready to go that far. There would be no compromising on this.

He hung his head then whipped it up when a thin arm slithered over his. Sabrina tucked herself good and close, leading him out the door and toward his doom.

The wildest ideas ricocheted through his mind as they walked. He could run away with Heather and make a new life. Somewhere away from his father. Away from the pack.

His wolf growled in disapproval. *We need both! Heather and the pack!*

Maybe he could start a new pack in unclaimed territory. Maybe he could try the relatives on his mother's side. Out in California, where his sister Carly lived. They all hated his father; surely they would grant asylum to him.

He was so wrapped up in desperate escape plans that he didn't notice when they crested the hill overlooking the ranch. Didn't notice Sabrina closing in on him until her mouth was glued to his. If he hadn't squeezed his lips tight, she'd have tongued him right down to his spleen. Jesus! What was she doing?

He jumped back, wiping his mouth with the back of his hand then scrubbing it on his jeans. "Don't you think we ought to get to know each other a little?"

"Sure, I'd like to get to know you better, Cody," she purred, shooting a hand toward his crotch. He caught it a hair away from his zipper. "In fact, I feel like I already know you."

*I doubt it.* Though he kept the words inside, his face must have given him away, because Sabrina's face went from puppy-dog perky to pit-bull malice in one cold-blooded blink.

That's when he realized it. This was not just about him. Offending the daughter of the Westend alpha meant jeopardizing his entire pack. She'd go crying to Daddy, who'd come screaming for revenge. Cody's father had toiled over a lifetime to forge alliances, making bitter sacrifices of his own. One wrong word and he'd set off a new feud. And judging by the little he knew of Sabrina, the only right words were *I do.*

Classical music floated up from the schoolhouse below: that yearning song, the one with the violin, striving to break free. Never had the notes sounded as bleak as they did today.

Damn his father! Couldn't he at least have asked?

Vaguely, Cody felt Sabrina—persistent little leech— thread her arm through his again and snuggle into his shoulder. It took everything he had not to recoil. She pointed down the hill with an exaggerated sigh, right to the spot where the old smokehouse used to stand. "Your dad said he'd build us a big house, right over there."

His stomach did a 360. That spot? That was Heather's—his and Heather's! It was the exact spot he'd secretly tagged for their future house. His imagination had already filled it with green-eyed, champagne-haired kids and a big, goofy dog. And Heather, always Heather. Only Heather.

Jesus, how the hell was he going to get out of this? One by one, his vital organs started shutting down. There was no out. His gut told him as much, even as it heaved. His eyes darted over the view of the ranch. What had always seemed an endless landscape now squeezed in like the walls of a cell.

That hill right over there, that's where the rogues had come in a few years ago. To the east was the spot where Ty and Zack had fought off outsiders looking to steal a mate. And over there was the highway, a symbol of the human world, whittling away at the edges of their territory.

He took it all in, shoulders slumping. His duty was here.

He tried telling himself he'd be no good for Heather anyway. She didn't know his true nature and never would. They just weren't meant to be. Even if the thought killed him, he knew his outer shell would keep ticking for another few centuries, no matter how hollow he got inside.

Blood mired in his veins as his heart stuttered and slowed. When Sabrina nailed him with another kiss, he willed his mind blank, even though the taste of her snuck in. Wrong, this was all wrong. Inside, his soul was kicking and screaming, but outside, he was frozen, lost. By the time they made it back down the hill, Sabrina was practically skipping in triumph while Cody dragged his feet.

"Cody, I need you now!" Ty barked, shooing Sabrina toward the council house with a look of distaste. "Kyle called. There's a new break in the case." He grabbed Cody's shoulder and pulled him aside then dropped his voice to a gritty whisper. "I swear I didn't know Dad was up to this."

The words trickled to his ears from the far end of a tunnel. "Doesn't matter," he muttered. "It's for the best." He hauled himself into this truck, feeling gravity triple. The gears moaned as he ground them into reverse, backed out, and headed for the highway. Duty called. No matter how his wolf protested, one thing would never change. He was his father's son, and duty came first. Always.

A glance in the rearview mirror showed Ty, jaw set hard. There, Cody told himself, he'd done it again. Seemed no matter how hard he tried, he always managed to let someone down.

Including himself.

# Chapter Sixteen

Heather had practically breezed through the school day. A glorious week with Cody—okay, a glorious week of nights. . . and mornings—with Cody, and she was glowing. She'd found a new kind of calm with him, despite all the uncertainty in her life. An inner calm that came from the sensation of two hearts beating just inches apart. A glass half-full kind of feeling she'd never had before.

Hell, her glass was more than half-full. It was overflowing, at least when it came to the physical. Cody had devoted a good quarter of an hour to her breasts on Wednesday night alone, until she'd woven her fingers in his dewy hair and guided him down to lap at her sex. She'd never trusted a man to do that before, but with Cody—well, there had been a lot of firsts. Ecstasy like she'd never known before this week hit her at the first flick of his tongue. When he popped his head up to check on her a minute later, his lips glistened with the taste of her, and she could swear the word that popped into her mind came from him. *Mate.*

Afterward, she nearly blurted it out. *I love you, Cody.* It seemed ridiculous, because how could anyone fall in love that fast? Clearly, she was just infatuated, right?

Something deep inside her laughed out loud at that one. They had fit enough emotion into the past two weeks to fill two years. No one had ever made her feel so complete. Just the quiet companionship of him sitting nearby when she went through the kids' assignments in the evenings was the stuff of her dreams. But she didn't dare say it, lest she break the magic spell. Instead, she tapped it into his skin, a kind of lover's Morse code. Three slow taps: index finger, middle finger, ring finger. *I. Love. You.*

One night at a time, he'd chased her nightmares away and coaxed out the part of her she had thought long gone. By the third night, she'd stopped triple-checking her locks and peeking out the curtains. Stopped waking in the night, drenched with fear. She remembered what life was like before. Life could be good. Life could be beautiful.

The heady feeling he gave her carried over into her days. She felt taller, freer, as if she'd doubled her yoga time or swallowed a magic pill. She'd even started humming, for goodness' sake! Like she was doing now, while the music played and the kids settled down for reading time.

Giggles brought her attention to the back of the room. Timmy had found something outside the window even more interesting than the adventures of Captain Underpants. Heather fixed him with a firm look and went back to her papers, secretly replaying Cody's kisses, again and again.

Timmy snickered. "Cody's got a new girlfriend."

Her head snapped up, mortified that the kids had picked up on her and Cody. Had she somehow let on?

But no, that wasn't it because eleven little heads were all swiveled to the window, looking up to the rise, where Cody stood locked in tight mouth-to-mouth with a curvy brunette half his size.

"Cody's got a new girlfriend—again," Timmy added, making everyone laugh.

Everyone but Heather, whose heart was free-falling through her chest. She could picture it, flip-flopping, desperately clawing for a hold.

"Cody's got a girlfriend," a singsong voice rang.

"Cody's got a girlfriend," the rest chimed in.

*Cody's got a girlfriend,* Heather thought, sick to her soul.

∞∞∞∞

Somehow, she made it through the day then beeped at every damn car on the highway all the way home. She parked abruptly, slammed her front door, and then collapsed in sobs on the couch. She'd read somewhere that the human body was 60% water, and now she knew, because most of it was flooding her face as she made inhuman noises, curled up in the tight ball. *Cody's got a girlfriend...*

She'd retreated into a heap in bed by the time a knock sounded on the door. A knock she'd jumped in anticipation of every night, like one of Pavlov's pathetic dogs. How naïve could she have been?

A second knock came, and all her sorrow, all her self-pity, formed a sharp arrow and took aim. She stomped to the door, flung it open. There he was, the scum!

Only he didn't look like scum. He looked like Cody, sweet and sincere, but anguished, too. Maybe... Maybe she should hear him out. Maybe—

"Heather—" he started, but stopped when his phone sounded from his pocket. The new girlfriend? Heather's face went hot. The man was a master of deception. She would not fall for him again!

"Wait—" Cody tried, but she beat him to the punch, gripping the door hard and slamming it in his face. Not a second chance kind of slam; a goodbye slam. She stood still, listening to the house shake.

A moment later, a timid knock. She opened the door to find a confused-looking Cody. Hurt, even. Well, she was the one who was hurt. Mortally wounded was more like it.

"Heather, I need to—"

She didn't want to hear what he needed. She slammed the door again, and this time, she was shaking as much as the wood.

A third knock, and her blood boiled over. Enough of him! She threw the door open.

"Baby, I—"

Baby? She was no baby. And he was no man. He was a coward, a liar.

"Get lost!" she screamed, right in his face. "For good!" She followed up with a slam that almost took the door off its hinges.

They were through. She'd never thrill in the simple sound of approaching footsteps again, nor wake up feeling so fulfilled. She'd never feel that sense of completion in being with someone else.

Because there was no one else for her. Just him.

She leaned against the door, half hopeful for a fourth knock. She knew she wouldn't have the strength to stand him up again; she loved him too much. But she was tired of letting other people rule her life. People who made her fear, people who made her love. The latter were nearly as bad as the former. So she would be strong. The old Heather would take charge of her life again and find some way to soldier on.

"Heather..."

His whisper carried through the door, accompanied by a light tap, then another, and a third. *I. Love. You.* Everything inside her heaved as she pushed her hands to her ears. Heather knew she was imagining it, wishing too hard for something that would never be.

Outside the door, his phone rang again. The girlfriend. God, how could she have been so gullible? There was a moment of silence followed by an echo in the floor—the faint tread of his step. Never mind that it sounded dull and dejected; she couldn't allow herself to care.

She buried her head in her arms, trying to muffle the sound of Cody leaving her life.

For good.

# Chapter Seventeen

Heather tried to settle down to grading papers to get her mind off Cody's betrayal but couldn't focus on anything but the pain. She should have known better. He was too smooth, too perfect. And far, far too experienced. A cowboy, a player. What did she expect?

Having already cried a reservoir of tears, she decided to try anger. Yes, that would do it. Anger was much more conducive to accomplishing anything. She forced herself to turn to work, powering up her laptop, only to watch it shut down. The battery was drained—a little like her—and she'd left the power cord at school. She slammed a hand down, making the table shudder. No way could she wait until Monday, not with six grade levels of literacy benchmarks to juggle.

*Fine, damn it!* She would just drive out to the ranch and pick it up.

On the way out the door, she cast a wary eye at the crescent moon, low in the sky. Never mind that she'd been discouraged from driving the ranch road at night. This was school business, right? She'd breeze in, grab the power cord, and breeze out. No one would even notice she was there.

She drove with the windows down, letting the cool night air scour her skin. There was so much space out there, so much earth and sky. So much regret, stretching to infinity.

A truck with its high beams on tailed her all the way. Couldn't they just pass? Heather cursed it then cursed herself and then Cody. She cursed his sunny good looks, his tender touch. Cursed the little boy hidden in the man. He probably didn't even want to be free, not when woman after woman willingly opened her legs and heart to him. He was probably off with that brunette right now, the new goddess on his altar. Heather was over in the discards pile, among so many weeping statuettes.

Eventually, the steady rumble of highway gave way to the rattle and grind of dirt road: the song of the ranch. Heather drove on until the car gave a sudden lurch. The wheel pulled left and the rhythm changed to roll, roll, thump.

A flat. God, could it get any worse? She banged a hand on the wheel. Dammit, if she could drive with a broken heart, the car could survive a flat. Let it suffer a little, too.

The car groaned along for a miserable mile before she let it roll to a stop. Any farther and she'd destroy the rim, if she hadn't already.

"Just great." She killed the engine and sat, fuming. She was in the middle of nowhere in the middle of the night with a flat, while crickets chirped cheerily outside her window. She heard something slither into the night and watched a tumbleweed somersault past, mocking her immobility.

Fine. She'd changed tires before; she could change a tire again. Calling for help was a lost cause. There was no reception on this stretch of road; everyone on the ranch complained about it. Anyway, who would she call? Cody? She snorted. *Cody, could you peel yourself away from your new girlfriend for five minutes and help me with a flat? Pretty please?* The only merit of that idea was the possibility of slamming a few more doors on him.

She stepped into the cool night air, leaving the headlights on. Shrugging off a shiver, she pulled her field hockey stick from the backseat. Never know when you might come across a rattlesnake, she figured. Plus, she could hit the tire with it, and possibly Cody, if he happened along. She hugged herself, eyeing her surroundings. Beyond the narrow strip of headlights was an abyss of darkness. Who knew what might be out there? Squeezing her stick tighter, Heather approached the tire and kicked at it. Nothing doing.

She was just popping the hatch for the spare when the whine of an engine registered in her ears. A truck had just crested the rise, coming from the highway.

She breathed a sigh of relief and tucked the stick behind her back. Holding it seemed silly now. With someone to help, she'd be on her way in no time.

With one hand, she blocked the glare of headlights, wondering why the driver didn't put the things on low beam. The vehicle slowed then stopped. Some kind of fancy SUV, that much she could tell. Everyone on the ranch drove dusty pickups that were never as waxed and polished as this one. After a weighty pause in which the wind seemed to creep away and hide, the driver's door opened. A tall, angular man stepped out, and cold instantly gripped her bones.

Suddenly Heather didn't want help any more. She wanted to jump back in the car and drive away, flat or no flat. But it was too late.

"Good evening," the man said, words slicing the night. He was stepping forward now, eyeing her. His long hair was black as fresh tar and just as shiny. He'd fit in at a trendy city bar but not out here in the desert. And instead of the scent that went with his look—the scent of a pricey cologne—the man carried the faintest odor of ammonia.

"Need a hand?" The voice matched the rest of him: slick, almost oily. Not to be trusted.

She gripped the stick behind her back and stammered a reply. "No thanks, I've got it."

He circled around the front of her VW, barely glancing at the tire before taking up an attentive stance at the front bumper. Heather spun at the sound of a click behind her and watched the other doors open. The SUV disgorged three more men and rose on its axles, relieved of its burden. A faint vibration, a disturbance flooded the evening air, making her skin crawl. Two of the men were tall and slight, rough copies of the first. The fourth was a vision straight out of her nightmares. He moved with confidence and calm, his skin sickly pale in the black and white exposure of night. The man was evil, through and through.

She took a sharp breath.

"A pleasure to see you again, Heather." Alon's voice slid over her body and seemed to tuck in behind her, nudging her closer. She wanted to run, but her legs were rooted to the spot, already agreeing to star in tomorrow's crime statistics. Because that's the only place this encounter would end.

"I've been looking for you for quite some time." The moonlight caught in his teeth, and she saw the glint of a fang.

Sick realization washed over her at his words. The man had hunted her all the way across the country, obsessed. She held back the scream building in her throat and sent out a silent SOS instead. As if anyone could hear. Bitter words reared up in her mind. *Cody, could you just peel yourself away from your new girlfriend for five minutes and help me with a vampire?*

# Chapter Eighteen

Cody had never done that before—slid down a door in utter dejection, right down to the floor. It was like a new yoga move—the kind that harbored no hope. So many beautiful nights at Heather's house, and now this.

He whispered her name into the doorframe, then tapped in the code—the one he'd been imagining meant *I love you.* He strained his ears for an answering tap, but nothing stirred inside. She'd slammed the door on her heart.

There. Yet another person bitterly disappointed in him— and this before she even found out what he really was.

*It's for the best,* a hollow voice lectured as he gathered his limbs and stumbled back to the car. Duty called. Literally. Because Kyle was bombarding him with a third urgent call in the last five minutes. Cody cracked his jaw, hard. Maybe that would help: covering pain with pain.

He knew what he had to do—wrap up the case with Kyle and get back to his old routine on the ranch. Heather's contract was due to run out soon, and then she'd be gone. He'd mate with Sabrina, produce a few pups. He would try to love them, even if he never loved her, and try not to think about what might have been.

Duty. So what if it killed him inside?

He checked his messages. *New victim. Meet me. Mile 13, Copper Mine Road. Kyle.*

The wind whipped through the open window of his truck, scolding him. Trying to focus on the case was impossible, though. A lifetime of driving wouldn't put Heather out of his mind.

Copper Mine Road wasn't far from Heather's place. A blaze of lights shone at a lonely spot along that lonely road. The crime scene. Three patrol cars, as well as Kyle's unmarked vehicle, were clustered around a compact car, parked well off the road. Cody parked but made no move to get out, struggling to remember why this was important.

*Because a woman has been murdered. Because solving this case might finally win Dad's respect.* The second reason didn't resonate with any of the wreckage inside him. The first, well, it was too late to help this woman, but the crime scene might yield some clue that would finally let them nail the vampires.

He got out of the car grudgingly, and it seemed like a long, long way down.

Kyle stepped up, face grim. "Another one. Happened last night, but only discovered now."

Cody followed him, ducking under the crime scene tape to the car parked under a thorny copse of mesquite. The driver's window was open, all doors ajar. The police officer standing watch over the vehicle was pale.

"Same profile," Kyle said. "Female, late twenties. Multiple knife wounds." *Sucked dry,* he added, for Cody's ears alone.

*Puncture wounds?* he asked, feeling the itch of his claws. He could already smell the ashy hint of vampire.

Kyle shrugged. *Her throat was slashed deep enough to cover up, same as the others.*

The vampires had struck again and covered their tracks. From where Cody stood, he could see the woman's torso, her torn and bloodstained clothes. He ducked in for a closer look and stopped cold.

It wasn't Heather, couldn't be Heather. That didn't stop his heart from flipping over, though. She looked enough like Heather for his stomach to clamp down, hard. The bun, the hair coloring, the general description all fit. "Jesus," he whispered. Too close, the resemblance was too close. Cody whipped away from the scene. Then he froze and rotated slowly back, taking in the car: a rusty orange compact, just like Heather's.

Cody backpedaled, stumbling for his truck. "Kyle, get in!" He jumped behind the wheel while Kyle stepped over, far too slowly. "Get in the fucking truck!" he yelled, gunning the engine. He took off as soon as Kyle had one foot in the door. By the time Kyle closed the door, they were going fifty and climbing.

"Uh, Code...?" Kyle started. His spiky hair echoed the surprise in his face.

Cody's hands bit down on the wheel to stop the shaking. "She looks just like Heather."

"Who's Heather?"

Cody ignored that. "Last victim was close, too. And the car was the same. Orange import."

Kyle was eyeing him closely, putting things together as Cody hit seventy, aiming for eighty, if the truck would let him. It was all he could do to keep his claws from ripping through his skin. Vampires were after Heather. He didn't know why or how, only that he had to get to her now. He took a hand off the steering wheel to punch her number into his phone. The truck swerved, screaming over rumble strips before he jerked it back on course. He had to know she was okay. Even if she didn't want to talk to him, he had to know. Had to get to her, right now. He'd pick her up bodily if he had to, take her to the ranch and keep her safe until he found the vampires and scattered their ashes all over the Southwest.

But the phone just rang and rang.

He hung up and tried again, desperately willing her to pick up. She had to be home, right? The truck rattled in agony. Still no answer. He threw the phone down and glowered at the miles between him and her house. "The New Mexico victims— what kind of cars did they drive?"

Kyle gave him a blank look. He shook his head then pulled his phone out and dialed. Cody reached for Heather in his mind. They said mates could find each other, even over vast distances. He shook his head at himself. What a fucking test.

He reached out with his mind, forming a warning. *Heather, lock yourself up. Heather, hide. Heather—*

Kyle grunted and clicked his phone shut. "Both victims drove hatchback imports. Orange."

His grip nearly broke through the steering wheel. Where the hell could she be?

# Chapter Nineteen

"So beautiful, so afraid." Alon's voice was aged honey; it flowed, but didn't taste quite right.

Fear rattled Heather's bones, but she shoved it away. She had to be strong, angry. Because anger was much more conducive to accomplishing anything—like saving her own skin.

"I'd like to see you on a road at night, outnumbered. Would you be so tough then?" She did her best imitation of a sneer.

Alon chuckled. "That's what I love about you, Heather." His tongue caressed the word love. "So strong inside." He came a step closer and sniffed the air. "So delicious. No one else comes close," he murmured, and her eyes went wide. Alon must have caught that because his stare pinned her like a butterfly to a display. "Cathy was a great disappointment, you know."

Her heart jackhammered in her chest. Cathy had suffered a terrible end, while Heather had escaped. But not this time.

"Oh no, have no fear. You're too good for that."

She glanced around at the other men, impassive automatons awaiting a command. What would it be? Kill? Rape? Cut? Her legs trembled as she scanned desperately for some escape. Did she have any chance of outrunning them? Of fighting back? Any chance at all?

Alon beckoned with his hand, calling her to heel. The man had some kind of magnetism because she nearly took a step toward him. But she caught herself and sent another silent plea into the night. If she could stall long enough, maybe someone from the ranch would drive by.

"I won't hurt you." His voice tried to soothe, but the icy edge gave him away.

*Right.*

"Be my companion, Heather." His fangs showed again. "You'll be a queen."

Her stomach recoiled.

"Come with me, Heather."

*Over my dead body.* She almost said it aloud, but why tempt a vampire?

He gave an exaggerated sigh, closing the distance between them. "I'm getting tired of waiting, Heather. If you won't give, I will take." He took a final step.

She shifted her feet, pulled out her hockey stick, and swung with all her might. Never had she put so much power into a hockey stick before. Then again, she was swinging for her life. Too late, Alon's arm jerked up to try to block it. The stick connected with a sickening crack, splitting his left cheek and throwing him to the right. Heather gasped and jumped away, but then froze in awe of what she'd done. The other three vampires did the same, lunging forward then halting in their tracks.

Alon had caught himself with one hand. The other was on his cheek, which was split wide open. She could see strange, red-blue blood pooling over bone.

The vampire rose slowly and took a long minute considering, tasting his own blood. The dark eyes that slid toward her were pure malice—enough to finally spark the impulse to run for her life. Her legs hammered into action, desperate to get away.

Behind her, Alon hissed two words. "You die."

Fear fueled her legs, enough to give her a head start. She made it to the edge of the road before the first vampire loomed, a dark shadow over her left shoulder. She lunged right, spun, and struck blindly in pure survival mode. The hockey stick connected with an unholy *thwack* that vibrated in her hands. She didn't stop to see where she hit him, though the man's grunt reported a solid blow. But not enough, and certainly not enough to shake off all four.

A few more steps and she'd be diving headlong into the night. The vampires were behind her, reaching out while she ducked. Instinct told her they'd crush her neck the instant they made contact. She ran on, desperate to at least die trying, not standing like a sheep. Not that anyone would know the difference once she was gone. Who did she have to miss her, anyway?

The night air shimmered before her, the way it did in the heat of noon. Something was rushing in from the depths of the desert, hell-bent on her. She skidded in her tracks. Were there more vampires out there?

An urgent whisper—the hoarse scratch of a bush, maybe?—told her to duck. It came as a command, and her legs complied before her mind could analyze it. She dove at the feet of the oncoming foe just as it leaped, a dark mass hurtling out of the shadows. Something brushed her back and she hit the ground hard, her hockey stick wrenching her wrist. Behind her, the road exploded in violence. She rolled, scrambling for rational thought.

*Get to the car!* cried another disembodied whisper. *Get to the car!*

She struggled to her knees. The car was right over there, the hatch opened as she'd left it. The road was a blur of sound and shadow as the vampires clashed with the beast that had come out of the night. All fur, fangs, and fury, it bellowed in rage and slashed with bladelike claws. It was a coyote—a huge one. She'd never seen anything like it. No, she corrected herself as it lurched past the headlights—a wolf. A massive, outraged wolf. Something flashed in the blur of the melee, and she froze at the sight of gold-brown eyes.

*Get to the car, Heather!*

The wolf drove the attackers toward the SUV. Heather forced herself to circle behind and inch toward her car. If she could lock herself in, she might stand a chance. Stick in hand, she rushed for the door, only to be body checked into it by one of Alon's men. All the air was pushed out of her lungs; her ribs screamed. Spiked fingernails pierced her neck, jerking her head back. Her stick was useless, trapped between her and the metal. The smell of ashes invaded her nose, along with the unmistakable scent of death and decay. She squeezed her eyes shut as a hot breath huffed into the back of her neck. She was trapped, helpless.

As the outer tip of a fang pinched her skin, something akin to the roar of a freight train thundered in her ear, and she was hurled away, bouncing off metal and earth until she came to a rough halt by the front tire of her car. Everything was a blur, a rush of sight and sound, permeated by a musky smell. Her eyes opened to legs—many furry, canine legs. She was trapped by wild dogs—no, wolves.

There was a chorus of growls, a scream, and then, the vampire before her fell. The wolves were on him in a deadly pileup of flesh and fur. Heather crab-walked backward until she bumped into the tire, struggling to comprehend what was happening. Who was attacking whom?

Two wolves kept her hemmed in against the car. Growls lowered to snarls as they turned their rumps to Heather, forming a living barricade. The tan-colored wolf immediately before her had long, lanky legs. Beside it was another, the darkest tint of brown.

Beyond them was a battlefield where the first wolf raged— the one with golden hair and a nick in one ear. Two vampires ripped at him with claws, fangs, and a blur of speed. Two more wolves stood over the fallen vampires. One wolf had spiky fur and a crooked tail. The other was a giant, bigger than any of the others by a good hand. Brown-black, like the night. Intense. He was watching the fight, growling. Why didn't he help the sandy wolf, the one taking on the last two vampires? That wolf was locked in the fight of its life, already matted with blood. Why wouldn't the others step in? Why didn't they do something?

Without thinking, Heather pushed between the two nearest wolves, holding her hockey stick high. Her mind registered that it was insane, but her body moved forward, intent on a suicide mission.

A growl, a shove, and she was back against the car. The nearest wolf rumbled in warning.

"Why don't you help him?" she shouted. "Why don't you help?"

The wolf tipped its head this way and that, those deep, dark chocolate eyes trying to communicate. The second one shook its ruff.

She stared. They wanted her to understand something. She tilted her head at them. What? That it was the golden wolf's fight, his chance to prove himself—was that it? She glanced up then away as his jaws closed on the neck of one vampire. At the same moment, Alon jumped him from behind, fangs bared.

The others stepped closer as if to intervene then stopped when the sandy wolf shook himself free and whirled to face his enemy. One-on-one now: the wolf against Alon, whose eyes glowed white with a malicious fringe of red.

She wanted it to be over. Wanted it to end. But she couldn't, wouldn't back away in the middle of this fight for her life. These wolves were somehow familiar. They had come to her rescue. If vampires could exist, then...

She winced at a death blow that crushed Alon's neck then shut her eyes against the rest. After moments of sickening tearing sounds, the road fell into silence, broken only by heaving breaths. When she looked again, the sandy wolf was swaying, his head dipping, struggling to stay on his feet. Gold-brown eyes found Heather's, the nicked ear twitched, and she knew.

*Imagine a pack of dogs,* Tina had said. *Better yet, wolves. Our guys are a lot like that.*

"Cody," she whispered.

Cody was a wolf. Those were his eyes beseeching her. Those were his limbs creaking forward, step by pained step. Suddenly, it all made sense. The clan-like organization of the ranch. The fierce privacy. The territorial instincts.

"It's you," she mumbled.

The other wolves parted, sniffing Cody and whining in concern. Ignoring all of them, he shuffled forward until his nose was almost touching her toes. He lowered his belly to the ground and regarded her warily. Her move.

Every eye seemed trained on her. Her mind was frozen, but her body acted on instinct, carefully crouching and slowly offering the wolf one hand, palm up. He sniffed. She reached farther and touched the only patch of fur not drenched in blood.

The wolf closed his eyes and let a huge volume of air exit his lungs in a long, grateful exhale that prompted one of her own. She ran her hands over him then cupped the huge muzzle. It was him, all right. She could see it all in the eyes. Boy. Man. Lover. Wolf.

"Cody," she managed, her voice trembling.

Just when she thought she might lose herself in those eyes, a commotion broke out nearby. A different wolf loped onto the scene, and everyone tensed.

Heather yanked herself out of her crouch and lunged forward, stick at the ready. No way was she going to let anyone touch Cody now.

The new arrival, a grizzled old wolf, strode up to her, snarling dismissively. The beast had to outweigh her by a hundred pounds. She tightened her grip on the stick and found herself tempted to snarl back, driven by an alien instinct to protect as Cody struggled to his feet.

The gray wolf's eyes stabbed her with their intensity. He growled, but Cody growled back. The brown wolf with the sparkling eyes let out a grunt. Heather stared. Was that Tina? The giant one that was muscling in close, taking up position at one side could only be Ty, and the long-legged wolf standing beside him—Lana?—seemed coiled for action.

It was a standoff of some kind: Cody was being challenged by the old wolf. That much, she could tell. The others were clearly in support, but let him face his own battle. *Damn them their pride!* Tension coursed off every wolf on the road as Cody's tail whisked left then right, swatting her legs with the measured strokes of a pendulum. *Mine. Mate.* The desert echoed and amplified the words.

"Hasn't he done enough?" she cried, throwing the accusation at them all.

The grizzled wolf stared, measuring her up. She stood stiff, gripping her stick, wondering where reality stopped and the desert started. Ready to swing at anyone who dared challenge her wolf.

Her wolf. She must be insane.

Cody was leaning heavily against her calves by then. He was clearly on his last legs, but he wasn't giving up. God, when would anyone cut him some slack? She clutched her stick tighter and leaned forward, willing the old wolf away.

Finally, he heaved the weary sigh of a martyr, turned with an angry twitch of his tail, and padded into the night, grumbling. Heather let out a long, slow breath and wobbled as headlights sliced the night and footsteps—human and canine— drummed the road. The latter sniffing and licking each other, the former kicking the vampires' ashy remains.

Then it was just her and Cody—wolf or human, she couldn't care less right now—wrapped in a tight bundle of fur and flesh. For a long time, all she did was breathe him in. Eventually, though, a woman's voice whispered and hands guided her to her feet. The next thing she registered was sitting in the back of a truck, hugging Cody close. Human Cody, wrapped in a blanket, murmuring her name.

"Heather..."

Maybe she'd just dreamed it all. She'd had a flat tire, and somebody had come to pick her up. There had been no vampires, no fight. No nightmare on a deserted country road.

Much as she wanted to believe that, one look at Cody's face told her a different story.

"Let me explain—" he started, voice cracking.

"Not now." She clutched him tighter. Words wouldn't make this any less crazy or any more real. She tightened her hug, willing her body heat into him. Closing her eyes to a world she wasn't ready to see.

# Chapter Twenty

Heather made it through the next three days, hunkering down in Cody's house, alternatively despairing over his wounds and marveling at the speed of his recovery. She made it through his explanation of wolf ways—how they shifted forms, how mates forged a blood bond with a bite, how pack hierarchy functioned. And how it was changing. The older generation was slowly learning that the new one would not accept their matchmaking games. There was no new girlfriend.

"There's only you," Cody said, pulling her close.

She even made it through the community dinner on the third night, where a hundred pairs of curious eyes turned to her as one. She pulled up short in the doorway, even as Cody squeezed her hand in pride.

"It's not every day they see the human who stared down my father."

Her face must have betrayed her uncertain response because Cody whipped back to the hall.

*Eyes down!* he thundered out a mental command that even Heather obeyed. Out of the corner of her eye, she could see him scanning each and every face for submission. Only then did he relax and squeeze her hand again.

"Hey," he whispered, "it'll be okay. You'll do great."

She wasn't so sure about that. Wasn't sure about anything, actually. She leaned in close, more for support than to whisper. "You can do that? Give a roomful of people a mental command?"

Cody pursed his lips. "Guess so. Never done it before."

She could swear the man stood half an inch taller after that, but the unwanted attention made her cringe. Cody covered

107

her hand with both of his and kissed her knuckles even as her nerves continued to flutter anxiously about. He led her to the head table at end of the hall, right beside the massive stone fireplace hung with antlers and knobby chunks of wood that the desert had sculpted into art.

Soon the room went back to a quiet murmur, everyone studiously ignoring the new arrivals. Everyone except the school kids, who bounced and waved. Cody made for what must have been his usual seat to the right of Ty, at the head of the table. But Ty stayed him with a grunt. Their eyes locked, and Heather sensed mutual respect pass between the brothers. Then Ty jutted his chin toward the unoccupied seat at the opposite end of the table. The other head, so to speak.

Cody's mouth cracked open and a second ticked by. Then he took a deep breath and sidestepped to his new seat, pulling out a chair for Heather on his right. She sank down, eyes on her feet, wondering if she would ever fit in to this world. For all their human ways, wolf hierarchy barreled through, loud and clear.

Cody was uncharacteristically quiet as Tina, Lana, and Rae took over with light conversation that covered everything but vampires and wolves. Little Tana helped lighten things up, too, showing off her food art: mashed potato carvings and green bean smiley faces. Heather was just starting to relax when she saw Cody's father enter the hall. She sank in her seat, praying the man wouldn't come to their table.

Tina patted her hand, reading her alarm. "Don't worry; he sits with the old curmudgeons over there."

She made it through all that, a baptism by fire into the inner circle of the wolf pack. She made it back to Cody's house afterward, calm and collected. Then the reality of it all exploded in her mind. *Vampires. Werewolves. Cody. Mate.*

Don't worry?

That's when she lost it and ran from the house, insisting Cody drive her home—her own place, back in the human world. She passed the excruciating drive with her head buried in her arms. Her mind was ready to shatter; her heart wouldn't be far behind. Cody started to follow her into the house, but she pushed him back out and shut the door in something just under a slam. She couldn't help it; her body was shaking that hard.

And he was gone. Sort of. She could swear she saw the shadow of a wolf patrolling the street after that. She drew the curtain on it. There. She had her peace, her space again.

The reality, though, was crushing.

For the next two days, Heather cried, flailed, pretended. She kept every door and window locked against the outside world and all the supernatural beings she didn't want to understand. She hugged herself against the pain of knowing it would never work. No matter how much she loved Cody, it would never work.

In the wee hours of the third day, she shoved her few possessions into the car, left a month's rent on the kitchen counter with no forwarding address, and fled. Aiming to escape, fast and far. A replay of her flight from Pennsylvania, blind and desperate.

She drove and drove as if an unseen enemy were still on her tail, heading west so fast, she wondered if she'd run out of continent before the urge to flee was satisfied. But slowly, gradually, her mind collected itself and her foot eased off the gas pedal. Eventually, she pulled over to a stop and turned off the engine. She sat in silence, staring at the landscape, letting the grandeur of the desert soothe her. What was she doing? Closing her eyes, Heather reached deep inside.

When she'd fled the East Coast, she thought she'd lost everything.

When the vampires caught up with her in Arizona, she had been a hair's breadth away from losing her life.

But she hadn't lost anything, except maybe her ignorance. She'd found, instead. A new life. A good man. A tight-knit community.

So what exactly was she running from?

A breeze made the nearby bushes dance and wave, drawing her attention to the landscape that had fascinated her from the very start.

A minute later, she gunned the engine to life and made a measured turn east. Her breathing steadied along with her pulse as she followed an inner compass, and every mile filled her with certainty. By sunset, she was wiping the last tear from her eye and gazing up at two overlapping circles, swinging in a friendly breeze. There it was, the ranch brand, hanging proudly above the gate. She turned her face to the streaked sky with a faint smile.

This. This place was home.

The music led her right to him after she parked the car and wandered a few steps—east, toward the schoolhouse. Toward a familiar, yearning tune.

It was getting dark quickly, but the schoolhouse lights were on. When she got closer, she pulled up in the path. Something was different. There was half a pile of shingles by the corner and a ladder propped against the roof. The walkway was different, too. The scattered gravel had been raked into a neatly delineated path lined with solar garden lights that spilled cones of light at her feet, inviting her onward. Slowly, she stepped closer, swung open the south side door, and stepped inside, holding her breath.

Her pulse beat harder as she looked around the room. There was no one there, but someone had been in recently because the music was playing, the lights on. And something was new here, too.

Slowly, she picked out the changes, flushing a little with the discovery of each one. The dusty old blackboard was gone; a brand-new whiteboard stood in its place, facing the classroom. The water cooler wasn't dripping any more. The back right window with the broken pane had finally been fixed, and over on the left...

She got stuck on the next breath. The crooked bookshelf was gone, and an unused desk had been taken away to make space for an aquamarine rug and two beanbags—one green, one blue. A treasure chest stood in the corner, propped open to show the books inside, and the wall was painted with an undersea scene, including... Yes, an octopus reading eight books. She covered her mouth with one hand because it was just as perfect as she'd imagined it. The kids would love it. Even Timmy might sit still in a reading nook like that.

She wanted to plop down on a beanbag and let it all sink in, but that would have to wait for another time. Because her gut was still churning, anxious to find her mate.

*Mate.* It had a certain ring, now that she'd had a chance to chew on it a while.

She continued out the north side of the room, back under the stars. It took her eyes a moment to adjust to the dimmer light, but then she found him. Cody—sitting on the far end of the porch with his back to the wall and his head tipped back like he'd been counting stars. But maybe he'd given up because his eyes were closed, and there was a beer in his hand. A cold drink at the end of a busy day, she guessed, judging by the amount of work done on the schoolhouse. She stepped off the porch and circled around to face him, her heart prancing and whinnying like an excited filly.

But something was wrong. He was uncharacteristically quiet and didn't seem to hear her approach.

"Cody," she whispered then cleared her dry throat and spoke louder. "Hi." A lame greeting for a moment like this, but her brain wasn't functioning properly just then.

Cody's eyes slid half open after a moment of quiet, and his reaction took her by surprise.

He lifted the beer bottle in a little toast. "Hiya, Heather," he said in a voice that was flat, emotionless, and very tired. Then his eyes closed again.

And that was it.

Heather's heart crashed. Was she wrong about everything? Was he mad? Was he—

And then Cody went on talking as if he'd never left off. "Christ, now I see you when my eyes are open." He shook his head hopelessly. "I see you when they're open; I see you when they're closed. I see you when I'm sleeping..."

A searing ache went through her when she realized what he meant.

"I see you day and night." He winced. One hand waved in the air as he squinted up and down her body then hugged the bottle to his belly and shut his eyes tighter than before. "And now I'm talking to you like you're really there."

Her knees wobbled, her hands shook. "Cody, I am here."

"Jesus, I can even scent you. You slay me, woman." He shook his head then slumped, and it gutted her.

"Cody, I love you."

His eyes opened but the blue was dull and gray. "Yeah, that's in my dream, too." His smile was sweet yet so sad, she could have melted on the spot. "You say that and a whole lot of other beautiful things I could hear over and over again. You look at me like you can see inside. You touch me..." He ran a broad hand along his thigh then let it flop abruptly to the ground. When he continued, his voice rasped. "You say you'll never leave me and our forever starts today. And I believe it every fucking time."

She wanted to drop to her knees and hug him like a sobbing child on the playground, but her joints had all locked up.

"Cody, it is me."

"Right." His voice was bitter, his eyes firmly shut.

What else could she say? What would he believe? She scanned the playground, so quiet now at sundown. Normally, it was filled with a dozen excited voices: Becky, with her bubbling laugh. Timmy and his jokes, always grinning ear to ear the way she was sure Cody must have done as a kid.

"Hey, Cody, you want to hear a good one?" she asked on impulse.

Cody let out a sour chuckle that said he was humoring his imagination. "Sure."

"Where do ghosts swim?"

He didn't say anything, but his fingers went tighter around the bottle.

She rushed ahead with the punchline. "Lake Erie."

Cody didn't move.

She let out an exaggerated huff. "Am I going to have to tell you second-grade jokes all night? It's me, Cody. It really is. Cody, I want you. Please."

His lips tightened. So he remembered that line, too. "You want me to what?"

His whisper was a replay of their first night together, and the words alone were enough to send a heat wave through her body.

"I want you to love me back," she said, as sure and clear as she could make it so he would finally believe.

Though his body didn't flinch, she saw every muscle tense. Then his eyes snapped open like a light had gone on.

So she said it again, all in a rush. "I want you to love me back. To take me back. To let me say sorry and beg you to let me try again. To listen and learn and figure out—"

He leaped up in one impossibly swift move and buried her in a hug that had no beginning and no end. The air went out of her, but it didn't matter, not just then. The two of them were hugging and kissing and crying so hard, she couldn't tell whether the tears were hers or his. Cody was murmuring something, over and over. She was explaining and promising and pleading while the crickets broadcast happy tunes into the night.

When she finally pulled herself together again—at least enough to start thinking about putting together more than a breathless mumble—he was cupping her face in two hands, his eyes damp and shining. "Christ, I thought you were gone."

She pulled him back into a hug. "I swear you'll never have to think that again."

They stood hugging for another minute before their bodies started to melt into each other.

"You can dance to this music, you know," she whispered. It was Verdi, and opera, but with Cody, anything was possible.

"Oh yeah?" He let one arm slip lower and slid the other higher without releasing his just-dare-me-to-let-you-go grip.

"Yeah," she nodded, drying her tears on his sleeve. "Let me show you."

She swayed right then left in the first steps of a dance she never wanted to end.

"Gotta warn you," Cody whispered. His lips tickled her ear. "I have two left feet."

She shook her head because every step he took was just right. His hips snug against hers, his shoulders round and strong, his hands holding her tight. And the only inner voice she heard was the one telling her this was perfect.

"The left foot is mine," she managed, and if her voice was husky, her heart was soaring like a kite. "The right foot is yours. We're made for each other, you and me."

He took over the movement and led her in a slow circle. All she had to do was rest her cheek on his and enjoy, etching the moment into her mind. A moment she'd tell her grandkids about someday.

"I've always loved this song," Cody murmured after the yearning music peaked, then wound down. "What's it about?"

"This song? It's about a special place."

He arched an eyebrow. "A place like this?"

"Home." She nodded with her nose right up against his chest to breathe him in. "It's a song about finding home."

He let out a happy *humpf*, like he'd known it all along.

# *Epilogue*

*Eight Months Later...*

A classroom was never more gloriously silent than the hour after the kids had waved goodbye and sprinted off into summer. Heather wiped the whiteboard, ending the school year. A familiar step sounded behind her, and two strong arms circled her waist.

"How's my girl?" Cody murmured, kissing her cheek.

"Good." She stretched the word out over several syllables, though it still didn't capture how good *good* was.

His hands patted her protruding belly. "And how's my other girl?" His voice caught when he said it, and she had to take a deep breath, too. Him and her, in for the long run together. It was magic.

"Cody! We don't know that it will be a girl."

"A bump that beautiful could only be a girl."

"That's sexist."

"Okay, how's this: a bump that intelligent can only be a girl."

"Better," she chuckled as his lips worked her neck, close to the spot where he'd marked her a few months ago. Still tender in a delightfully erotic way.

She turned in his arms. "We're both ready for summer vacation."

"Me, too." He kissed her again.

A bark, and Maxi ran in. A black puppy with oversized feet, and a worthy successor to good old Buddy, the best dog ever.

"Look." Cody scooped him up. "Aren't I a good dad?" He held Maxi close to his face, grimacing against a lathering of puppy slobber.

Heather's heart swelled. *You'll be a great dad.* Outwardly, though, she kept her composure. "Yes, well, Maxi doesn't need diapering."

"Do you know how many times I've cleaned the floor?"

She had to give him that one. He'd been sweeter than sweet these past six months.

"Lady, I'm gonna be Doctor Diaper," Cody insisted.

"You better be, once I get back to work."

"Three months. You get three months off work after the baby is born. And then the baby is all mine."

The man was too good to be true. "You're not planning to share?"

He set the puppy back on the floor. "Only with you." He took her school bag and slipped an arm around her shoulders.

Heather turned off the light and gave the room a last look. Arizona had brought her a huge streak of luck, one that seemed to stretch as far as the hills. Janice, the teacher she had been filling in for, had decided to stay in Ohio. The teaching job was Heather's, for good.

The man, too.

She tilted her head up to the sky as they walked, throwing out her gratitude to whatever gods had engineered all the good surprises in her life. It was a regular ritual for her these days.

They walked, sticking to the shade, taking their sweet time. A cardinal sipped from an irrigation ditch; leaves rustled overhead. The light breeze tasted broad and sweet; promising, even. Cody leaned into her side, steering her left.

"But home is that way." She pointed right.

He squeezed his lips in a mischievous look. The man was up to something, for sure. "How about the long way around?"

They took it, walking to the edge of the trail to let two oncoming trucks pass. Rae drove the first one with Zack beside her, both of them grinning a mile wide. Heather had to smile as she always did at those two. The stories she hadn't believed from the kids about midnight hunts and wild chases—they were all true. And the funny thing was, what had once seemed so outlandish was perfectly normal these days.

A second truck rumbled past with Lana waving from the front seat. Heather did a double take. "Wait—Ty didn't just wink, did he?"

"I told you my brother shows his soft side once a decade or so."

She snorted. Yes, Ty was a great guy, but he still intimidated the hell out of her. How two brothers could be so different... She wondered if her own kids would be the same, and then laughed out loud.

"What?"

She shook her head. No need to look too far into the future. The present was rich enough.

Maxi ran ahead and rolled in the dirt, grunting like a happy pig. Heather could have done the same, though she'd prefer to roll on Cody. Not that she hadn't had her share of that these last couple of months. They ambled on, letting the desert do the talking, until they turned a corner and slowed.

The house was right over there, a modest building with a grand view that started with pasture, swept past the hills, and extended to eternity. The house Cody's father was building for his retirement. Everyone had been pitching in for months now—hoping, perhaps, to hurry the man off the throne. Standing on a small rise on the east side of the community where the sun rose first, it occupied the very spot Heather would have picked for her dream house. Lucky for Cody's dad, he'd snagged the spot first.

Not that she was complaining. Cody's bungalow had quickly shed its bachelor pad trappings and become a snug home. Soon, they'd get started on the addition they'd put off while Cody worked overtime on his father's house. He'd been coming home late, sweaty, and strangely satisfied for a man who'd been laboring for someone else.

"It's done," Cody nodded toward the house, hugging her from behind.

She held back a sigh.

He squeezed tighter. "It's ours."

Her blood slowed, just a tick.

Leaning in, Cody whispered into her ear. "We weren't building it for my father. We were building it for us."

She caught her next breath, and the one after that, and the one after that. All the hours everyone had put in.... "For us?"

"Surprise."

Her house. Their house. The U-shaped ranch of her dreams. Cody had remembered, all the way back to the day of that geometry lesson in school.

The front door opened and Kyle stepped out, hefting a toolbox. She'd barely gotten to thank him for his role in tracking down the vampires. Looked like she wouldn't get a chance, either, because she could barely breathe, let alone talk.

Kyle tossed Cody the key and grinned. "Welcome home," he said, and though his voice was cheerful, his eyes were sad. He said *home* the way a color-blind man might say *rainbow*. Then he left quickly—half exit, half escape.

Cody tugged her closer to his side as they watched him go. He sighed a little, ruffling her hair. "A story for another day. Today is ours."

*Forever starts today.* Every time she replayed those words, she had to sigh—as she did when Cody led her inside, anxiously watching her reaction. The man gave her goose bumps when he did that—taking delight in her happiness.

He could have showed off and told her how hard he'd worked, how difficult it was. He had every right to point out all the details he'd sweated into place—the ornate window mouldings, the fireplace built by hand from local stone. But he didn't. She threaded her fingers through his as he led her from room to room. The man had so much to be proud of, yet he was still good old Cody.

Well, in almost every way. The jokester had been pretty well replaced by the man these days. A good man who knew when to laugh, when to buckle down, where duty started and where it ended. One who'd finally established his footing on his own terms.

Her man. Her mate.

He'd told her everything after that awful night of the vampires. Starting with his father arranging a mate to strengthen pack alliances. The old alpha had a twisted way of wanting the best for his pack.

Somehow, though, things had all worked out, thanks to Audrey. Yes, Audrey, the local man-eater. Heather still couldn't believe that turn of events. Audrey had transferred to the Westend pack in Nevada, declaring herself ready for a change of scenery and bemoaning the lack of eligible males at Twin Moon Ranch. She'd wasted no time in making a mate of Roric's oldest nephew. Thus both alphas were placated, even if Sabrina was not. Word was, she was currently angling for a mate in California. As long as the woman stayed clear of Arizona, Heather didn't care.

Cody was doing it again—rubbing the bite mark on her neck. She cooed under his touch. Scary as the mating bite sounded, it had gone just as he said, only better. They'd been on fire that night, making love as never before. The bite amplified the intensity, sweeping them to the climax of their lives. When they'd cuddled together afterward, he'd gently fingered the mark.

"You could have bitten me any time," she'd whispered, full of awe. "But you didn't. Why not?"

"That wouldn't be right. You had to want it, too."

"I think I wanted it even before I knew what it was." For all that wolves and mating bites had once scared her into leaving Cody, the only real danger had been her own fears.

And her first shift into wolf form? It started with a pulling sensation, her face stretching in a mighty yawn that traveled through her body like the mother of all yoga moves, fast-forwarded. Cody stayed right at her side, his fur brushing hers until she insisted on practicing four-footed coordination alone. When he came back from where he'd been hiding around a corner, just in case, they ran and ran and ran. Then they tried another new move: mating as canines. Not so different, except for the solid half hour of furry nuzzling that followed.

They ended that magical night in a ballad, Heather letting her wolf voice warble for the very first time. Until that moment, wolf howls had always sounded mournful to her. Now that she spoke the language, she understood. Yes, there was sadness, but the rest brimmed with promise, love, and, above all, hope.

From hilltops all around them, the voices of her packmates chimed in. Her pack. That feeling of belonging she'd lacked all her life was finally hers.

Like the house. Cody leaned in close, brushing away the tears that welled up when they finished the tour and crossed the threshold back into the living room, a soothing world of beige and cream tones. Her yoga mat was already propped in one corner, and a bowl of strawberries beckoned from the granite counter. The photo of Buddy stood on the mantelpiece, beside the one of her and Cathy, with space around them for all the memories still to come. Maxi ran between them, sniffing like a hyperactive vacuum cleaner.

"The party starts at six," Cody said, catching her in a hug.

"What party?"

"Our housewarming party. Tina insisted. But she said not to worry. She has it all organized, even the cleanup."

Heather sniffed as her heart swelled. Being pregnant and desperately grateful made for a potent emotional cocktail.

Cody's hand inched down her rear. "How about we do our own housewarming?"

She covered his lips with hers and mumbled a yes. A fire was already raging within her, insatiable for him. "Party's right here, mister. Right now."

Locked deep into her kiss, Cody tapped an answer on her back. One, two, three.

She tapped right back.

*I. Love. You.*

∞∞∞∞

# Other books by Anna Lowe

## The Wolves of Twin Moon Ranch

Desert Hunt (the Prequel)

Desert Moon (Book 1)

Desert Wolf 1 (a short story)

Desert Wolf 2 (a short story)

Desert Wolf 3 (a short story)

Desert Blood (Book 2)

Desert Fate (Book 3)

Desert Heart (Book 4)

Happily Mated After (a short story)

Desert Yule (a short story)

Desert Rose (Book 5)

Desert Roots (Book 6)

# Serendipity Adventure Romance

Off the Charts

Uncharted

Entangled

Windswept

Adrift

# Travel Romance

Veiled Fantasies

Island Fantasies

visit www.annalowebooks.com

# Sneak Peek I: Desert Fate

Kyle Williams is just a lone wolf trying to settle in to a new skin. But when the brown-eyed girl from his past turns up, bloodied by a rival male, the instinct to protect overrides everything else—including duty to his pack.

Stefanie Alt is a woman on the run, and fate is hot on her heels. The only one who can help her is the neighborhood bad boy she once knew. But even after one hot night under the desert moon, Stefanie isn't sure she can trust him—or herself.

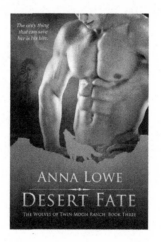

# Sneak Peek II: Chapter One

Stefanie lay belly down in the dirt, vaguely aware of the first tap of sunlight upon her back. The wound on her neck throbbed, a reminder of the madman who set off this nightmare. The nightmare that had brought her to this place.

When she cracked one eye open, the red rock landscape was glowing orange-pink with dawn. She sucked in a long, unsteady breath, and it seemed like half of Arizona was squeezed into that lungful of air because her head spun. The place was like old leather: dry, worn, and rugged, yet rich and textured at the same time. Gritty and alive.

A little like her. Gritty. Alive, if only just.

She was going mad now, too, imagining all kinds of crazy things, like sprouting fur and claws and howling at the moon. Driving at breakneck speeds across two states hadn't helped outrun those crazy thoughts, nor had it shaken the feeling of being pursued.

Going to the police wasn't an option, much as she was tempted to try. If they heard the truth, they'd check her in to a mental ward. She could play it all out in her mind already.

*What seems to be the problem, miss?*

*I was attacked.*

The cop would nod, reach for a report, and wait for more.

*I was attacked by a man with two-inch fangs who growled and grabbed me and—*

That's when the officer would tear up his report, pick up the phone, and ask for the psych ward.

No, going to the cops was not an option.

She licked her lips, trying to assemble her scattered thoughts, but they all kept coming back to two words.

*Skinwalker. Wolf.*

Two words aimed at her not far past the Colorado-Arizona state line. She'd pulled over at a trading post after driving like a banshee for hours, desperately thirsty and bone tired. When had that been? Yesterday? The day before? She couldn't remember. Only that she'd made straight for the water fountain, hoping the shadows hid the mess she had become. Her hair, her clothes—all of them a mess. At least she'd had a shirt to change into. One that wasn't covered in blood.

She still wasn't sure how she'd survived after losing that much blood, but all that had mattered at that moment was the feel of cool water sliding down her throat. She barely caught the nod of greeting from the old Navajo woman who sat hunched over some beadwork in the shade—but she couldn't miss it when the woman suddenly jolted off her stool and backed away, her eyes wide in horror.

"Skinwalker..." The ancient voice rasped with fear.

Stefanie snapped away from the fountain and put her hands up in protest.

"Wolf..." the old woman murmured, clutching at her robe.

Stef stammered and stumbled until she was back in her car. Then she peeled out of the parking lot and sped away. But even as she drove—going sixty-five, seventy-five, pushing eighty—the words kept echoing in her mind.

*Skinwalker. Wolf.*

It was sunset—a few hours and several hundred miles later—before she'd calmed down enough to pull over. She'd stared at her knuckles, locked white around the wheel, then tilted her chin up to study the stars. That, she remembered exactly. The sky, blood red around the horizon, deep indigo overhead. The cool evening air. The rattle and whoosh of cars racing by. Where was she going? What would she do when she got there?

She traced the hook of the Big Dipper then the W of Cassiopeia with her eyes. For all that had gone wrong in the past few days, the stars looked exactly right tonight.

Then she did a double take. Wait. Hadn't they looked better from about a mile back?

*I am definitely losing my mind.*

No one could sense that small a change. But there was a hush in the air that stopped her from shaking the idea away. Like the desert had whispered something and was waiting for her response.

Something like, *That is the way you must go.*

So, okay, she made the U-turn. If instinct told her to follow the stars, she'd follow the stars, no matter how crazy it seemed. What else did she have to lose?

A mile later, an unmarked road split away from the highway and an upward glance told her that the stars really did look better from here, if still not exactly right. So she bumped down the dirt road, checking the stars every few minutes.

They did look better from this angle, part of her insisted, and for a little while, that part took over. Every mile she drove took her closer to...

To where?

To wherever it was that felt right. It was like a blindfolded childhood game where you honed in on something: warmer, warmer...

Then the right front tire blew out and hissed its anger into the night. She groaned, dropped her forehead to the steering wheel, and stayed there a long time.

No one could help her, not even the cops. And now, she was stranded in the middle of nowhere in the middle of the night. How could she have thought there was anything right about this?

A coyote yipped in the distance then broke into a long, warbling howl. For a minute, it sounded vaguely... familiar. So much that she was almost tempted to sing along. Tempted to toss her head back and let out all the frustration, the pain, the fear. To disappear into the desert and hide in a den.

When the coyote trailed off, loneliness came crushing in along with the crazy images that had started plaguing her at night. Images of running into the night like a wild thing. Of howling her sorrow to the moon through a long, pointed snout. Of tearing something fleshy apart and tasting warm, sweet blood...

She fumbled with the door handle and jumped out of the car as if that were the seat of her madness, and then rushed into the shadows of the desert. Faster and faster until all she heard were her own hurried breaths, her own desperate footfalls.

It all became a blur until dawn, when she found herself belly down in the dirt, the sun tapping on her back. There was a rattle, and she glanced up in time to see the diamond pattern of a snake slithering by. Had he too, spent a frigid night on this mesa?

She was still flopped there, vaguely aware of the intensifying heat of morning, when an engine grumbled in the distance—the first vehicle to pass since last night.

*Maybe they can help!* Part of her wanted to believe that impossibility.

*No one can help,* the other part cried. *No one can understand.*

A good thing she was far enough into the bush that the driver wouldn't see her. She'd be left in peace, hopefully to die.

*I don't want to die!*

But some things were worse than death, so she lay still. If she was lucky, the sun would take care of what the snake failed to do. All she had to do was lie there and let her mind drift.

She should have known not to step foot on that Colorado ranch alone. Should have listened to the creeping doubts that had warned her away...

The cool earth under her cheek carried a vibration. Something was moving nearby.

A shadow fell over her, too tall for a snake or coyote, and she tensed. The touch on her shoulder was warm and broad. A human hand. With it came a human voice.

"Are you okay?"

The voice was deep and warm, and she wouldn't have minded listening to it all day.

But the cynic in her wanted to snort. Okay? She'd nearly had her throat ripped out by a maniac. Her dreams were nightmares full of canine sights and sounds. She'd been on the run for days. Okay?

*I've never been further from okay.*

Adrenaline coursed through her veins as the instinct to flee kicked in. With a lunge and a twist, she was up and running, crashing through the bush.

"Hey! Wait!" the man's voice, so soft a moment ago, shouted in surprise.

Like hell, she was waiting. She squinted as she ran, trying to adjust to the bright sunlight. Despite the stranger on her heels, running gave her a thrill, like that of a captive animal set free. She darted around a cactus, hammered up a slope, then skidded down the other side in huge leaps. But the air rushed behind her, and with it came the jolt of a flying tackle. Then she was tumbling and tangling with her attacker, both of them bashing into the hillside until they ground out against a rock.

"Ooof." The man groaned, then cursed. "Lady..." he started, then suddenly stopped.

He had her pinned on her back under his sheer weight. All she could see against the glare of the sun was his outline. It didn't take much for her imagination to fill in the features of a different attacker, a different man.

"No! Get off me! Stop!" She clawed at him wildly, trying to break away. She wouldn't let Ron get close! Wouldn't let him bite her again!

He pushed her back into the ground, hands firm yet careful. Confident. Controlled.

"It's okay. Listen, it's okay."

The voice was low and gritty, and that's when she realized that this wasn't Ron. This man stood much, much higher up the food chain. He was stronger. Smarter. Faster. A predator, not a scavenger like Ron. She could tell by the firm line of his mouth, the clear honesty of his eyes. The brightest pair of eyes she'd ever seen: summer blue shot with strands of gold, like the sun streaming through a cloud on the leading edge of a rainstorm. She found herself going warm all over, lost in the allure of that light.

If this was death—hell, she'd greet it like an old friend.

129

# More from Anna Lowe

Check out the other side of Anna Lowe with a series even die-hard paranormal fans rave about: the Serendipity Adventure Romance series. You can try it FREE with *Off The Charts*, a short story prequel you can receive for FREE by signing up for Anna Lowe's newsletter at *annalowebooks.com*!

Listen to what a few Twin Moon fans have to say about this new series:

- *This is as HOT as her shifter series. For those who want spicy without paranormal, this is a perfect start. I can't wait to read more about these characters.*

- *I'm enjoying Anna's new series just as much as I do her Wolves of Twin Moon Ranch series.*

- *It's not my normal genre but I do love Anna Lowe's romance books because of the great way she writes. I am really happy this book was the same great style.*

- *Uncharted is different from Anna's Wolves of Twin Moon Ranch but I enjoyed the story just as well.*

# About the Author

USA Today and Amazon bestselling author Anna Lowe loves putting the "hero" back into heroine and letting location ignite a passionate romance. She likes a heroine who is independent, intelligent, and imperfect – a woman who is doing just fine on her own. But give the heroine a good man – not to mention a chance to overcome her own inhibitions – and she'll never turn down the chance for adventure, nor shy away from danger.

Anna is a middle school teacher who loves dogs, sports, and travel – and letting those inspire her fiction. Once upon a time, she was a long-distance triathlete and soccer player. Nowadays, she finds her balance with yoga, writing, and family time with her husband and young children.

On any given weekend, you might find her hiking in the mountains or hunched over her laptop, working on her latest story. Either way, the day will end with a chunk of dark chocolate and a good read.

*Visit AnnaLoweBooks.com*

Made in the USA
Coppell, TX
21 May 2022

78014603R00083